Ghost Stories
of
Shimla Hills

Minakshi Chaudhry has travelled extensively as a reporter for *The Indian Express*. She has authored two books, *Exploring Pangi Himalayas: A World Beyond Civilization* and *A Guide to Trekking in Himachal*.

Ghost Stories of Shimla Hills

Minakshi Chaudhry

RUPA

Published by
Rupa Publications India Pvt. Ltd 2005
161-B/4, Gulmohar House,
Yusuf Sarai Community Centre,
New Delhi 110049

Sales centres:
Bengaluru Chennai
Hyderabad Kolkata Mumbai

Copyright © Minakshi Chaudhry 2005

Foreword copyright © Ruskin Bond 2005

This is a work of fiction. Names, characters, places and incidents are either the product of the author's imagination or are used fictitiously, and any resemblance to any actual persons, living or dead, events or locales is entirely coincidental.

All rights reserved.
No part of this publication may be reproduced, transmitted, or stored in a retrieval system, in any form or by any means, electronic, mechanical, photocopying, recording or otherwise, without the prior permission of the publisher.

P-ISBN: 979-81-291-0753-3
E-ISBN: 978-81-291-2139-4

Thirty-third impression 2025

35 34 33

The moral right of the author has been asserted.

Typeset by Mindways Design, New Delhi

Printed in India

This book is sold subject to the condition that it shall not, by way of trade or otherwise, be lent, resold, hired out, or otherwise circulated, without the publisher's prior consent, in any form of binding or cover other than that in which it is published

To
My brothers, Neeraj and Deepak,
for the bond of friendship

Contents

Acknowledgments ix
Foreword xi
Preface xv

The Angrez Churail 1

Haunted Roads, Bauris and Benches 7

The Spirit Takes Revenge 20

The Premonition 29

The Bhootwallahs 41

The Sanjauli Fruit Seller 50

Bhoot Bangla 58

The Road to Lovers' Paradise 67

The Ghost on the Railway Line	78
Enduring Love	85
Ghosts Don't Exist	96
The Walk Back	102
The Grave of an English Lady	109
The Prince with the Red Rose	120
The Lady on the Rickshaw	132

Acknowledgments

There is a long list of people who have directly and indirectly made this book possible. I acknowledge my sincere debt to all of them. I can say that collecting tales of real experiences and encounters is definitely not easy. As I wandered looking for these, I went through a lot of embarrassment, frustration, discomfort and anger. Thankfully the end product overshadowed all this.

My gratitude to all who narrated their encounters and allowed me to write them down, and thanks also to all who laughed and scorned at my endeavour.

It goes to the credit of my friends, Lalit, Deepshikha and Sunita, who listened to my progress regularly with patience and encouragement. Thanks are also due to the then Deputy Commissioner of Shimla, Mr Ram Subhag Singh, who intervened twice to prove my credentials when I landed in difficult and awkward situations.

I must add that the idea of this book was suggested by my teacher Vepa Rao to whom I owe a special debt of gratitude. I want to express my gratitude to my editor who tightened the stories to make them crisp and interesting, and to my publisher for publishing this work.

Above all I would like to thank Rakesh, my husband, for his unconditional support and help.

Foreword

It's good to know that Mussoorie is not the only hill-station with a generous sprinkling of ghosts. Shimla, it appears, has more than its fair share. Indeed, judging from Minakshi Chaudhry's entertaining collection of tales, there are almost as many ghosts as people parading on the Mall or under the deodars.

Kipling started it all with his phantom rickshaw and its ghostly occupant, and since then there have been any number of phantoms, of one kind or another, haunting Shimla's old schools, hotels, cemeteries and places of entertainment. In 1947, the British left the country but left their ghosts behind!

Countless sahibs and memsahibs, and sometimes their children, are known to reappear in their old haunts and homes, or in dak bungalows scattered throughout the land. It's high time we got these British revenants to quit India before they get up to further mischief.

The dak bungalow or forest rest house was and still is a favourite haunting-ground for long-dead British officials. Today, Indian Civil servants do not return from the dead with the same frequency as their predecessors; they look forward to a long rest from the problems associated with the administration of their districts.

I'm not sure why these ghostly variants favour old bungalows and rest houses. After all, no one lived in them for very long. Many years ago, trekking with friends from Shimla to Mussoorie, we had to stop for the night at Chakrata, where we were warned against spending the night in a certain forest rest house, reputed to be haunted by the malignant spirit of an Englishman. Sometimes he took the form of a black dog (with red eyes), sometimes he appeared as a large rat.

To avoid his attentions we decided to accept the invitation of a dhaba-owner down the road to sleep in his shop. In lieu of mattresses, we were provided with woolly sheepskin rugs. These kept us warm, but by midnight we were crawling with vermin. Armies of fleas (pissoos) had emerged from the sheepskin to feed upon us. Scratching, swearing, and unable to sleep, we fled from the dhaba and took refuge in the haunted rest house. We did not see any mad dogs or Englishmen. If you're dead tired, you won't see the walking dead.

Ghost-hunter Minakshi Chaudhry treats the reader to a variety of ghosts, British and Indian, rural and urban. My favourites are the churails, whose feet face backwards. In spite of this disability, they can run very fast in pursuit of their victims. To get away from a churail, try running backwards. They dislike eye contact.

I wish the reader a happy outcome to any encounter he or she may have with any of the spooks described in this charming potpourri of the supernatural. In the meantime, read and enjoy!

Ruskin Bond
September 2005

Preface

The fear of the unknown, eerie and the strange—enhanced by pattering raindrops, mist, darkness, thick deoder jungles and lonely forested paths—is part of life in the hills. I spent six months in 1999 wandering around Shimla hills; my aim was to collect as many stories as I could about British ghosts. Perhaps inevitably, I came across several tales about 'native' ghosts and spirits, which also find a place in this book. During my travels, I met people who claimed direct personal experiences with ghosts, and people who had heard these tales first hand. I spent many hours talking to these people, hearing the most fascinating tales of experiences and encounters with supernatural beings.

I did not meet a bhoot or churail face to face (thank god!). Although, truth be told, the supernatural beings I heard about were not always things to be feared— I heard of many friendly and helpful spirits. In fact, most of the ghosts, I found, were harmless and content to be among themselves.

All the stories narrated here are based on a core *belief*, which my sources swore to be true. My research was not a scholarly project, but was a result of interactions with people. Most of the stories, told to me by elderly people, go back to pre-independence when Shimla (then Simla) was the summer capital.

I have changed the names of the people involved as per their wishes. I also want to emphasise that I do not intend to hurt anyone's sentiments or tarnish the reputation of institutions. All I have done is tried to recreate an ambiance for tales that have circulated for generations.

Do ghosts exist? We do not know. Perhaps we can *never* really know. But yes, ghost stories do exist. And these tales are *real.*

The Angrez Churail

'Sadhu! I am coming. Wait for me.'

Sadhu heard the wailing tone following him. She even knows my name, he thought, panic gripping him. He did not look back. Trembling with fear, he tried to scream and run, but he could do nothing. His feet seemed frozen.

She was getting closer.

His mouth ran dry and his scream died deep inside him. His wobbly legs refused to move. Sweat poured down his forehead. 'O Bhagwan, bachao...I will offer 101 rupees to Ma Bhagwati,' Sadhu wept silently.

'Sadhu wait! I am also coming,' said the voice again, now closer to him. It was child-like, but it had an icy ring to it. He started sobbing, and made a last effort to move. He gathered his strength and finally his legs obliged. He ran towards the bridle path leading to his house. He felt her following him and looked back. Her face had changed beyond recognition: though still that of an angrez, it was distorted, and certainly not human.

Now he screamed and in fit of horror ran blindly. The thing, crying and laughing in the same breath, was nearing him. He felt her at his back, almost at his heels, but this time he did not turn.

He reached his house and wildly pounded on the door, banging it with his head, crying for help as he screamed. He fainted when the door opened.

That night, Sadhu's entire family could not sleep for a minute: the woman stayed outside their door, howling, screaming and laughing the entire night.

◆

I looked at Sadhu as he was telling me about his experience. He was trembling with fear even as he spoke. He was a short man, in his sixties, with a crooked, prominent nose. I looked at him curiously. 'My nasal bone broke that night,' he said, as if reading my mind.

'When did this happen?' I asked.

'Nearly twenty years ago. I stopped my business at Boileauganj after that and shifted to Chakkar. I do not walk in the dark on that road even now. It was a moonless night I remember...' he said.

◆

Sadhu is a roadside vendor who sold his wares near the bus stand at Boileauganj, a small suburb of Shimla town, about five kilometres from Scandal Point. The area got its name from two Englishmen: Col. Boileau and his younger brother. Both the Boileaus were known to be eccentric: the brothers had once received their Commander-in-Chief into their house standing on their head, with their legs up in the air.

Boileauganj is a junction from where many roads branch off. The main road connects Shimla with Bilaspur and other districts; one road turns left to Summer Hill where Himachal Pradesh University is situated; a broad path leads to Kamna Devi temple on Prospect Hill; and another road connects Boileauganj with Chakkar. Sadhu, who lives at Chakkar and took this road every night after work, had to pass through a thick conifer and oak forest.

The evening was like any other. There were very few people around the Boileauganj junction and the vendors were beginning to pack up their wares for the day. Sadhu had not started packing up his stuff as he was waiting for the last bus. Just then he heard the rickety noise of an approaching bus before its headlights blinded him. The bus stopped a few metres away from where he was squatting with his products. The other vendors did not stop packing up, though they looked expectantly towards the passengers.

A small group of men who had been strolling around the junction for nearly half an hour boarded the bus. An old woman got down from the bus, crossed the road, and took the path to Summer Hill. The bus roared off, passing them all.

'It is nine o'clock. Your long route bus has gone, now pack up. Is it not enough to have sold and pocketed money for the last twelve hours?' asked Jeet Ram, Sadhu's friend of many years.

'Well, it's just that when you all start packing, I get very confused. I'd rather wait for you to finish, so that I can do it in peace. After all, it is a matter of five or ten minutes more.'

'Stop bluffing. I know you well! You wait till we go so the last customer will come to you because we would have packed and gone off!' his friend joked. 'Anyway, see you tomorrow. Remember it's your turn to sit in the middle, I will take this place, as per my turn,' he chuckled. They had been rotating where they sat for years. Though it hardly made a difference as far as business was concerned, it was a good arrangement psychologically. Both of them felt that the person sitting nearer the bus stop attracted more customers.

In another five minutes Sadhu had also packed his stuff and, adjusting the fifteen-kilo tokra on his head, he started off. He was one of the few lucky ones to have a room close to his place of business, a mere fifteen-minute walk. The house had belonged to his elder brother, a bachelor, and it had passed on to him when his brother had died.

The path was shrouded in darkness. There was a slight October chill in the air. Balancing the tokra on his head, he pushed his hands into his pyjama pockets. Sadhu knew every curve on the road—he had walked it twice a day for more than two decades.

In a few minutes he reached the three huge water tanks. He heard the gurgling and thumping sound of water hitting the bottom of the tanks. Sadhu stopped to adjust the weight on his head when he saw a silhouette a few metres ahead of him. Surprised, he looked intently into the darkness. There was no doubt, someone was walking in front of him.

'Perhaps it is someone I know,' he thought and quickened his pace. As the distance between them reduced, he realised that the silhouette belonged to a woman. What was a woman doing walking alone on this lonely track, he wondered.

'Where are you going, all alone in the night?' he asked softly, so that his voice might not frighten her. There was no response.

'Where do you want to go? I am also going this way; my house is nearby,' he said again.

Still there was no reply. Annoyed, he tried again. 'Look, I am trying to help you. It's very unusual for a woman to walk alone late in the night. I do not have any other motive, I am a family man.'

Silence again.

By now Sadhu was walking alongside her. He could hear the shuffle of her feet. Something about the sound struck him as odd and he looked down. He could see her feet even in the darkness—they were white, thin and bony. She was not wearing any slippers and she seemed to be dragging her feet as she walked. He thought there was something wrong with her feet, but could not make out exactly what it was.

All of a sudden Sadhu realised what was wrong with them, and his mouth went dry. He started trembling as the full meaning of whom or what he was walking beside sunk in!

He knew about churails from his friends. And the way one could identify them was that their feet were turned inwards. Terrified, Sadhu looked at the woman's face. It was beautiful, and she was an angrez!

He was trying to figure out what to do, when he heard her say, 'Sadhu, take me with you.'

Haunted Roads, Bauris and Benches

Three A.M. on the Ridge. Rajesh is walking through the fog carrying his luggage. He has to catch a bus to Chandigarh, which is scheduled to come into the Shimla bus stop from Kinnaur in the next ten minutes. As he walks down the road, struggling with his bags, he notices a man in a long white robe sitting on a wooden bench a few metres ahead of him. Involuntarily he shudders as he passes the figure. There is something strange about him. The blank, distant look on his inanimate face, all yellowish in the muted street light. He feels an urge to leave his luggage right there and run for his life. He hardly covers a stretch of fifty metres before he musters the courage to look back. The bench is empty! The Ridge is empty! There is no one there. The man has just disappeared into thin air!

◆

The open ground in front of Christ Church is known as the Ridge. The crest of the hill was levelled in the nineteenth century, creating a fine area from where locals and visitors can enjoy a panorama of the northern snowy peaks and southern hills.

In 1855, before it was levelled, the Ridge consisted of a narrow street with a row of shops on either side; it was called the Upper Bazaar then. The bazaar was destroyed in 1875, when a devastating fire razed several shops to the ground. Rebuilding on the charred side was prohibited, instead, affected shop owners were provided compensatory sites on what is now known as Mall Road.

Though the final victory of the Allies in World War I was celebrated in 1918 on the Ridge, the gathering there was strictly restricted to less than 150 persons at a time. This restriction was imposed to ensure that the water reservoir below it would not suffer any damage from abnormal pressure.

Now, of course, the restriction is not adhered to. Hordes of people use the Ridge every day, unaware of the danger that they are posing to it. Independence and Republic Day celebrations, and rallies are held here with all pomp and glory with audiences running into the thousands. And that's not counting the ghosts.

The more you ignore the rumours that the Ridge is haunted, the more you encounter people with experiences such as Rajesh's. Many places in Shimla town, particularly the open roads, are also apparently haunted. Take for example Scandal Point. Unbelievable? Well what can I say.

People claim that if a person crosses Scandal Point between 2 A.M. and 4 A.M., he or she may have some strange experiences. Conversations in hushed tones, the sound of jhampans moving, the smell of perfume in the air, the soft tinkling of laughter intercepted with squeals of joy. And yet there is not one person visible.

A person who ran a popular restaurant on the Mall claims to have come across a British woman standing at Scandal Point, wearing a wedding gown. When he and his uncle, who was with him, passed by the woman, it occurred to them that it was very unusual for a woman to be standing there, at that hour, in those clothes. Later, his uncle told him that they had not seen a British woman, but a ghost.

◆

It is popular belief that the stretch between the Indian Institute of Advanced Studies and Summer Hill is haunted. The thick forest on both sides, dominated by oak trees, is lovely; but during the night, the atmosphere changes. Some students of Himachal Pradesh University claimed that they had met an Englishman wearing a hat and long overcoat here.

One student was stopped by this man near a rain shelter, fifteen minutes away from the university. The man asked for a cigarette. Being a non-smoker, he was unable to give him one. The student explained this to the man, and the next second he was slapped twice on the cheek. When he lifted his hand to strike the man for his audacity the stranger had vanished.

Apparently, the ghost also asks for a lighter; if you don't have one, he walks beside you silently for sometime and then disappears. He walks like an aimless zombie, and by the time you realise the strangeness of your unwelcome companion he is gone. If you do have a lighter or cigarette, and on his request you graciously offer them to him, he disappears immediately, in front of your eyes without taking either.

◆

The U.S. Club Road from the Ridge below the spur of the Jakhoo temple also has its own share of scary stories. It is said that sounds of the tapping of a walking stick and the canter of a horse are heard at night. People have heard the sound of a galloping horse and the swishing sound of a whip as it hits the horse in the Richmount area around midnight.

♦

The Forest Road, or Lovers' Lane as it is popularly called, is one other spot where British ghosts wander. An ideal place for cavorting teenagers because of its seclusion, there used to be five benches at the top of the spur.

Aman resides in the U.S. Club and goes for long walks along this road in the morning and evening regularly. This has been his routine for more than two decades. He is an artist, and the walks not only uplift him spiritually and make him physically fit, they also make him more creative in his work.

On one such evening, about a decade back, when he reached the somewhat flat portion where the five benches were, he stopped and decided to rest.

Admiring the beautiful vistas spread out before him, he was approaching the benches when he felt someone coming up from behind. Thinking it was someone else on a walk, he paid no attention but moved forward. Seconds later he felt someone overtake him. Unlocking his gaze from the mountain ranges he looked in front and then behind him. There was no one there. Puzzled, he sat down on a bench and got the shock of his life! He was sitting on someone's lap! With a shriek he jumped up, embarrassed. But the bench was empty, there was no one there. Then he felt cold, very cold.

Aman did not try and figure out what it was; he literally ran from the five benches. It was only after a few weeks that he could bring himself to cross the area alone again.

After that first experience, Aman has felt someone walking alongside him on several occasions when he passes the five benches. Though he has never had the courage to sit on a bench again, he has slowly gotten used to his eerie companion.

◆

When Vijay, now a leading businessman in Shimla, was fourteen and studying in the ninth standard, he had a bizarre experience here. He used to go for tuitions near the area. After his tuition, he usually took Mall Road to reach his home in Chhota Shimla. One day, on a whim, he decided to take the longer, lonely route past the five benches.

As he neared the five benches, he heard the distinct murmur of conversation. He could not make out what was being discussed, but he could distinguish different voices: there seemed to be more women than men.

Haunted Roads, Bauris and Benches 13

When he turned the sharp curve which brings the five benches into sight, he saw a group of foreigners sitting and chatting animatedly. There were about four or five women and two men. He did not think anything of it till he was about twenty metres away from the benches; it was then that he noticed that their hairstyles and clothes were quite peculiar. The women were wearing gowns, bonnets and their hair fell around their shoulders in curls. The men were dressed in breeches, and their hair was slicked back. Suddenly he began to feel cold. On an impulse, he decided to ask the group from which country they belonged.

In a few seconds he was just a few metres away from them. He felt uncomfortable and embarrassed as not one of them looked at him.

He stood there, unsure what to do. He felt a chill numb his toes, hands and the back of his neck. Ignoring it, he mustered up his courage.

'Excuse me, sorry for interrupting,' he said apologetically, and then paused. To his chagrin, not one of them turned towards him. It was as if he had not spoken! He decided to force them to acknowledge his presence.

'Didn't you hear me? I wanted to ask you from which country you have come,' he said, speaking loudly this time. The group did not take any notice, but continued talking to each other.

'Are you deaf? I am speaking to you foreigners!' he said angrily.

There was still no response. Behind him, he heard the purr of a car. Baffled and angry, he stared at the group for another second. He decided to stop the car and request the driver to question these people with their strange hairstyles and clothes. He turned and took a few steps.

Then, just to see if they had responded to his moving away, he looked back. There was no one on the benches! Not a single person! He stared in sheer disbelief as the car went past him.

◆

Located on the eastern end of Mall Road is the Marina Hotel, formerly the famous Glenarm Hotel which functioned as a ladies club (Zenana Kalaf) during the British Raj. Grass widows and unattached women used this hotel as a temporary or permanent place to stay in. In those days, there used to flow a spring which formed a small pond just in front of the club's entrance; the pond was believed to be haunted by a churail. It was said that the spirit enticed unwary travellers at midnight, particularly Englishmen; in the morning these travellers would be found lying unconscious nearby. The pond was later filled up and sealed with rocks and boulders and the spirit is said to have left the place in despair to some unknown abode. The spring which fed the pond dried up subsequently.

◆

It is still not clear to me who or what churails really are: were they women who practiced witchcraft? Or women who had died at the time of childbirth? No one seemed to know for sure, but I could gather many interesting tales about them. The accepted belief is that churails wander near water sources between 12 noon and 3 P.M. when the sun shines at its zenith, or from midnight to four in the morning. But descriptions about what they look like vary from beautiful damsels decked up in bright clothes, and badly applied make-up, and, on the other extreme, that they are monstrous creatures with protruding nails and teeth, with unkempt long hair. They can be identified by their feet and hands, which are turned inwards. Folklore has it that they change their form to appear as a woman, a man, a child or a beast. And they can only be seen by men.

There used to be several churail bauris in and around Shimla: urbanisation and deforestation have now caused many of the watering holes to dry up, and with them related churail stories. The most notorious churail bauris were at Combermere Bridge, Kunchums

Bauri below Ripon Hospital, the United Services Club Bauri, Boileauganj Bauri near the railway line, the Sanjauli Bauri and the bauri between Sanjauli and Chota Shimla on the National Highway.

Rocky and his friends were on their way back from Mashobra, eighteen kilometres from Shimla. They had just had a farewell party for him—he was leaving India soon to work abroad. By the time he dropped his friends at their homes in Dhalli and Sanjauli, it was two in the morning. Finally, only Aamir and Rocky were left in the van.

As they passed St Bedes Chowk, a lady suddenly walked out in front of the van, seeming to appear out of nowhere. Startled, Rocky slammed his foot on the brake. The tyres screeched as the van came to a halt.

'What the hell?' Aamir shouted.

As he heard the bewildered cry of his friend, Rocky looked up. There was no one. Oh God! he thought. I must have hit her. He pulled open the door and hurried to the front of the van.

The woman was lying on the road, facing him, just a couple of inches from the tyres. She smiled at him and he gave a sigh of relief. After all, who would smile after being hit by a speeding vehicle.

'Is she dead? Did you hit her?' Aamir's voice came over his shoulder.

'Can you get up?' Rocky asked her. She gave a small nod and then got up slowly. She was of his height, slim, beautiful, with long hair falling to her hips. She was wearing a saree.

'We're terribly sorry. I don't know how we didn't see you,' Aamir said, leading the woman to the pavement. He asked her if she would like to be dropped anywhere while Rocky inspected the van to check for any damage. Satisfied, he walked towards the two who were standing a few metres away.

Rocky felt a little uneasy as he looked at her. She was adjusting her saree, her long black hair falling about her face. Her beauty did not affect him, as it was obviously affecting his friend.

His uneasiness increased as he approached them.

'She wants to go to Chhota Shimla,' Aamir said.

Rocky looked at the woman. She didn't look at him, but a small smile appeared on her face, the same smile that he had seen when he had found her lying in front of the van.

Suddenly it struck him that there was something very odd about the whole situation. What was she doing there all alone in the middle of the night? And she didn't seem at all perturbed by the accident. The van could have killed her! Also, she seemed completely at ease with two strange men.

As Aamir led her towards the van, she walked past Rocky and their eyes met. Images of a sea of bones, skulls, snakes, long strands of hair, small children in pools of blood and old dishevelled women, their mouths open wide in laughter, flashed through his mind. He tried to look away or shut his eyes, but it was as though an unknown force had hypnotised him. And then, like it was being replayed, he could see her lying down on the road, her smile, her getting up, brushing her clothes and straightening her hair with her hands.

Her hands!

He jerked himself out of the trance and looked at her hands again. They were turned inwards.

Rocky caught hold of his friend and dragged him into the van as Aamir mumbled, 'What...what...'

'Leave her alone and get in you fool,' he screamed. He pressed his foot on the accelerator and drove blindly, clutching the steering wheel with all his strength. He ignored Aamir who was hurling the choicest abuses at him. He stopped only when they reached home. It was then that he looked at his friend. Aamir was lying unconscious next to him, with blood dripping from the side of his forehead.

◆

It was around midnight and Shyam was driving from Sanjauli to Chhota Shimla. His mind was on an important legal case, and he was driving at about twenty kilometres an hour. About 100 metres short of Churail Bauri, he saw a woman waving her hand, gesturing him to stop. She was clad in a red saree.

It flashed through his mind that she must have been attending a wedding because of the way she was dressed. He slowed the car and was about to stop when he saw that the woman was no longer there. He looked ahead. There she was. About a hundred metres away, now standing near the bauri. Baffled, he drove on, again slowing down as he approached her. She was now waving her hand frantically.

Shyam wasn't sure what he saw first—her hand or her face—but it made him drive away as fast as he could. Her hand was turned inwards, and her face had been terrifying—big red lips with long teeth protruding out. Her howls and screams followed him as he sped past her.

From that day, he has never travelled on that road late at night again.

The Spirit Takes Revenge

Major Longwood felt good as he settled down into the easy chair of the resthouse at Kaithu: he had managed to escape the blistering Calcutta summer. This was his third trip to Simla in the last two years since he had come from England. Calcutta was his headquarters; he was allowed sick leave once a year, in addition to the annual one month's leave. Being a well-planned man, he only fell ill in the summer, never in winter when the Calcutta weather was tolerable. This time, he had been given two weeks for recuperation and rest.

Longwood found the general atmosphere and climate in Simla similar to that of England, and that was the main reason he preferred it to any other hill station. He was particularly fond of this resthouse too. Most of the resthouses in Simla were located on the spur at vantage points, but this one was further down the hill. It was a comfortable double-storey house with half a dozen outhouses attached to it.

'Would you like to have some tea, sahib?' Birbal the cook asked him.

'No Birbal, come sit down,' Longwood said, pointing to the stairs on which the cook sat whenever he wanted to chat with him. 'Tell me, how have the last few months been?' he asked.

Three cooks and about a dozen servants were employed to take care of the guest house which was normally occupied the whole year around, except winters. On his first visit, the Major had struck a cordial and affectionate relationship with Birbal, who was nearly sixty-five years old.

'They went fine sahib! All days go fine,' Birbal said in his philosophical tone. Longwood laughed loudly slapping his thigh, 'Knowing you, I should have known the answer beforehand,' he said.

'Was it very hot in Calcutta, sahib?'

'Yes, very hot. What will you know about that weather Birbal? You have never gone out of this town of yours. Anyway, tell me what has gone on in the last six-seven months since my last visit.'

At Simla, as almost everywhere in India, the locals knew everything that the Britishers did, and they readily communicated their knowledge to their European sahibs.

'Nothing much, sahib. I am always busy here catering to other big sahibs. What will I know of the fashionable world?' he said respectfully.

'No, I mean the scandals, the rumours, the stories that went around. You have been watching us people for the last many decades. So you know our inner and outer lives,' Longwood said jovially.

Birbal smiled in his innocent way and shook his head, 'I don't know anything sahib. Lots of big sahibs like you came and went. Their memsahibs, so fair and colourful, chattered around like summer flowers. They went out in the mornings and came back late in the evenings.'

'You are a scoundrel, I will ask the other chap. What is his name...Ramu? Yes Ramu. He will give me a better and more detailed picture!' Longwood joked.

For the next few minutes both of them sat in companionable silence, looking out at the serene forest.

'There was one incident, sahib. However, no one could make head or tail out of it.'

'Well you can tell me all about it later. I forgot I have to meet a friend at the Mall. Will you bring me that cup of tea now please?' Longwood said.

◆

It was after nearly eleven that night that the Major settled down with a book in his bed. It had been a hectic day. The excursion to the Mall had been as entertaining as he had expected. However, the heavy dinner with that extra helping of caramel custard, which his hostess had forced on him, had made him feel bloated. He had skipped the cup of tea that he usually had after dinner.

Yawning, Longwood put the book aside, he had read enough. Switching off the table lamp, he adjusted the quilt around him, tucking it in from all sides.

But deep sleep evaded him. Through the night he had dreams about a girl, a fair pretty local girl, who kept on crying and moaning without saying a word. He woke up three or four times in the night with an overwhelming feeling of sadness.

In the morning, the feeling of grief stayed with him and he didn't feel like going out. He spent the whole day reading and dozing.

'Are you not feeling well, sahib?' Birbal asked respectfully when he brought the Major his after-dinner tea.

'I don't know Birbal. Nothing physically wrong with me, but I've been feeling very sad since morning,' he said.

'Something the trouble sahib?' Birbal asked, in a worried tone.

'No, no. Never mind, forget it,' Longwood said. After all, he himself could not understand why he was feeling this way. He had had a light dinner and despite Birbal's efforts to make him taste the dessert, he did not do so.

'Bring my cup of morning tea at five, please Birbal. All this lying low has made me lethargic. I'll go for a jog tomorrow,' he said.

After Birbal left, he read for an hour disinterestedly and then decided to sleep. He had switched off all the three lights in the room and was about to switch off the table lamp when he saw, in front of him, the outlines of a figure taking shape. He rubbed his eyes thinking it was a trick of the light, but no, a figure was definitely forming in front of him—it was getting clearer every second. In a minute, a girl who looked around sixteen was standing in front of him.

Oddly enough, Longwood did not feel any fear or terror.

'Who are you?' he asked, the incongruity of the situation not escaping him.

'I am Manju's spirit.' She had not spoken, but he understood.

Spirit! She was a ghost! Longwood thought, as he got up from his bed.

'I want you to take revenge for my murder,' the girl said.

'Murder? What are you talking about?'

'I was killed two months ago. I want you to take revenge.'

'Look, I don't know why you've come to me. If you are a spirit, as you say you are, why don't you take revenge yourself? You must possess more powers than me!'

Was he really talking to a spirit? Or was he dreaming? And then it struck him! The girl in his dream the previous night and the one standing before him now were the same! How could this be? And why wasn't he feeing scared or frightened.

'I have seen you before, I saw you in my dream yesterday!' he blurted out.

'Yes, I came in your dream. You have to help me sahib, you have to punish the guilty,' she said.

'Well...why don't you tell me your story. I'll decide after I hear it,' he said.

She was the daughter of a milkman, the girl said, and her marriage had been fixed with a boy in the adjoining village. Sometimes her father sent her to the resthouse with their daily supply of milk. About two months back, when she came to leave the milk ration as usual, an Englishman stopped her near the kitchen. He pressed himself on her. Frightened, she tried to escape from him, but he was too strong for her. She bit him hard on his right arm, but he did not let go. He dragged, and then carried her to his room, where he threw her on the bed. She opened her mouth to scream when a pillow was stuffed on her face and that is how she breathed her last.

Longwood was quiet for sometime.

'What happened to your body? What did he do with it?' he asked, not sure what to think yet of the entire story.

'He buried it.'

'Buried it! Where did he bury it? And no one saw him doing it?' he asked incredulously.

'He buried it in the bathroom, underneath the bath tub.'

'But...but how did he do that alone?'

'The bath tub was yet to be installed, sahib. He covered me with sand and cement and placed the tub on top. He supervised when the tub was being cemented permanently.'

Longwood stared at the figure. Was it the truth?

'You believe me, sahib, don't you?' she asked sadly.

'I just don't know why you aren't taking revenge of your murder yourself. I have heard that spirits do that,' he said lamely.

'It is not only revenge I want, it is justice. My disappearance has brought shame on my family, sahib. I want everyone—my father, the villagers, my fiance—to know that I was murdered. I want my murderer to face trial and be punished for what he did to me,' she finished with dignity.

Longwood looked at the trembling figure and knew that she was telling the truth.

'Who was your murderer?'

'Your junior sahib, Michael Saab.'

'Michael!' Longwood said, startled.

Michael, the nineteen-year-old boy who had just come from England. He had committed this gruesome crime? When had he come to Shimla? Busy with his thoughts he did not notice when the figure of the girl disappeared. 'Hey, where did you go?' he called out to the empty room. 'This is too much!' he said loudly, and then he remembered—she was right, he had granted Michael two weeks' leave around two months back.

He had another sleepless night. When Birbal came with his tea early the next morning, Longwood related the incident to him. 'Oh, that is what I was going to tell you the day you came sahib,' Birbal said. 'The milkman's daughter disappeared suddenly—everyone thought she had run away.'

Over the next thirteen days, Longwood tried to get some action taken in the case. He lodged an FIR in the Boileauganj Police Station and filed a case in court. At night, Manju's spirit would appear before him and he would discuss the case with her.

When the case came up for evidence, he told the shocked judge that the spirit of the victim would come and give her evidence as there was no witness to the murder apart from herself. And, as Longwood said she would, the spirit did come into the judge's chamber and recited exactly what had happened with her to the astonished judge. Later that day, the bath tub was removed and Manju's decomposed body was found underneath. Michael broke down and confessed to his crime.

This building, along with the outhouses, was dismantled a decade back. There is a Trishul and a small Shiv Temple near the site now.

The Premonition

It was quiet, almost unnaturally quiet.
The tall trees loomed darkly overhead, not even a whiff of air disturbing the stillness. A fog had suddenly descended, reducing visibility to near zero. The environs had an evanescent quality that seemed a natural and integral part of the strangeness of the place. A little later, the gaps in the atmosphere filled up as the thick clouds of fog gently swirled around becoming softer, cotton-like. The catalyst for this transformation was the whispering wind. It had silently come and taken everything in its fold in just a few seconds. Nothing could be seen, except for the soft clouds which had joined together to make a smooth unwrinkled space for themselves.

'This is called mist. Have you ever seen anything like this?' the woman asked courteously.

Raveena was in no mood to make conversation; until the middle-aged woman had spoken, she hadn't even noticed her arrival. She was too busy thinking of her situation.

'No. I have come here for the first time. It is somewhat new,' she said. She couldn't very well have ignored the woman.

'They say during the British Raj, people who were sick and wounded were brought here to recuperate,' the woman said.

'Ya, I read that somewhere.'

There was silence. How could anyone get cured here, Raveena thought. It was so deathly quiet, eerie and suffocating.

'It was nice meeting you. You will be good company. Good-bye,' the elder woman said.

'Same here. Perhaps we'll meet again soon,' Raveena said politely.

The woman looked directly at her. 'It will be sometime before we meet. But you may come across my daughter soon,' she said slowly, and then walked off, disappearing into the mist.

Raveena stared at the whirling mist into which the woman had disappeared, not knowing whether to be relieved by her departure or surprised by her behaviour.

'Ah! There she is. Come here Raveena, let me

introduce you to your teacher,' her father said beckoning her.

'Well, I won't be teaching you but we will meet on and off. I am in charge of the hostel,' said the nun as Raveena reached them. Raveena almost extended her hand to shake the nun's hand, but as an afterthought restrained herself. Perhaps she wasn't supposed to shake hands with teachers here, unlike Australia. So instead she said a muted hello.

This seemed not to have been the right thing to do either, she thought, as she noticed the nun assessing her with cold eyes.

Her father did not notice her discomfort, but then, he hardly noticed anything concerning her. A few moments later he left her with the stern looking nun.

'Would you like to ask me anything about the college?'

'Er...no. Except, if you could please tell me the way to my hostel room? I don't think I will be able to find it on my own with all this mist around,' she said, staring helplessly at nothing in particular.

Sister Margaret had been apprised of the girl's background by her father. He had told her that his daughter was a shy, introverted girl who seldom made friends easily. She was likely to dislike the college, and even fear it for at least a few months. This was what worried him, he told the nun: Raveena was intelligent, but her insecurities lead to what he thought were baseless fears. This was why he had decided to bring her to Shimla.

'I'll take you there,' Sister Margaret said briskly. 'This foggy weather will remain like this for a long time. It is always like this during the rainy season. You will get used to it.'

It took them a few minutes to reach the hostel from the administrative building. The nun left her at the hostel's entrance and it took sometime for Raveena to find room number 23. She knocked at the door. 'Ya, come in! It's open!' a voice answered.

Feeling self-conscious, Raveena opened the door; it was a medium-sized room: there were three beds, and a study table near each bed. A large window faced the door.

'You seem to be looking at the room as if it is yours,' the room's occupant said. The girl was sitting cross-legged on one of the beds.

Raveena entered, closed the door, moved towards a bed and sat down.

'I think it is your room!' the girl said sheepishly.
'Yes.'

'Hi, I am Sandy. Short for Sandhya. I'm from Jallandhar. And you must be Raveena. Our other roommate was here a few minutes ago, she has gone to bring her luggage.'

Sandhya was a fair girl with prominent freckles on her face. She had come two days ago and had settled herself comfortably with all her things—clothing, toiletries, books—stacked in one of the cupboards. She had even pasted posters of her favourite hero Aamir Khan on the wall adjoining her bed. A pink fluffy cotton stuffed dog with long drooping ears sat beside her on the pillow. Five pairs of shoes had been neatly lined up under her bed.

Stroking her stuffed dog, Sandy studied her roommate with curiosity. Raveena was of medium height, with a thin frame and a wheatish complexion. Dressed in a yellow T-shirt and jeans, she was not beautiful, but she had an intelligent face. She seems shy, Sandy thought. Apart from that one 'yes', she had said nothing. Her hands were tightly clasped, her eyes glued to the half-open window.

'Where is your luggage? Didn't your parents come to drop you?' Sandy asked, trying to start a conversation.

'I just have a small bag, the rest of my luggage will come in a few days. My father will send it from Delhi.'

An awkward silence followed.

'How come you knew my name?' Raveena asked at last.

'It's written on the notice board. There are only four girls who have been admitted in the final year: us, our other roommate, and a fourth who is sharing a room with her sister who is in second year.' Sandy paused, then asked, 'Are you not happy about coming here?'

Raveena kept quiet.

'So you are not happy coming here. Our other roomy too is not excited. As for myself, I'm okay. I like the place and the weather...but if I'm going to be stuck with you two unhappy creatures...!' Sandy laughed, and then, noticing the expression on her roommate's face, anxiously asked, 'What's wrong?'

'You like the weather! The college building is fine, but the place—the mist, the thick black jungle, the looming trees, I feel...I feel trapped. I hate it!'

Before Sandy could reply to Raveena's outburst, the door opened. A tall thin girl, staggering with the many bags she was carrying—a suitcase in each hand, three bags dangling from her shoulders, and one hanging round her neck—stood at the door.

'It's your room. Don't just stand there with all that stuff. Put it in the corner,' Sandy said, gesturing towards the right side of the room.

The girl walked in, raised her right foot to shut the door and then stumbled forward letting the luggage drop in the middle of the room with a thump. She grinned good-naturedly at Sandy.

'Raveena, Mini, our third roomy,' said Sandy cheerfully introducing one to the other.

'I think we've met before,' Raveena said hesitantly. She felt as if she had seen the girl somewhere before, but she couldn't quite recall where or when.

'I don't think so...I don't remember meeting you before,' Mini replied tentatively. 'Where are you from?'

'Delhi, but I did most of my schooling in Sydney. I studied in India for three years, then left again, and have just come back now to complete my graduation,' Raveena explained.

'How long were you away from India the second time?' Sandy asked.

'You mean in Sydney? Two years.'

'There was a gap in your studies?'

'Yes. I was not well,' Raveena said quietly. She looked at Mini, trying to recollect where she had seen her. Perhaps it had been at the airport?

◆

Over the next few weeks, Raveena's initial fears gradually decreased. She still felt uneasy when she was left alone, but that was not often. She had struck up a strong friendship with her roommates, and life became almost normal for her. But she was still not comfortable with the mist.

It was a month after her arrival that she saw the place where she knew she would die. She felt like a fool: for so long she had seen this place in her dreams, and here she was, practically knocking on the door of her own death.

It was an outing day, when the girls were allowed to leave the college campus till eight PM. The three of them—Raveena, Sandy and Mini—had gone to watch a film at the Ritz. It was a thriller; she did not enjoy it much, but her friends loved it. They had a late lunch at Fascination Restaurant and decided to walk back to the hostel via the Sanjauli route; it would be about five kilometres from the Mall. By the time the friends had had tea at Pappi's Dhaba, the sun had set and it was getting dark.

Both Mini and Sandy were brisk walkers and Raveena had to make an effort to keep pace with them. After some time, she lagged behind. When they were about half the way to college, she saw the woman that she had met on her first day at college coming from the opposite direction. Raveena stopped as the woman approached her. Her friends went on ahead: they did not seem to have noticed the woman although she walked right past them.

'It's nice to see you happy. Do you like my daughter?' the woman asked as she reached Raveena.

Raveena was confused. The smile on the woman's face did not reach her eyes. She was so well dressed, not a single strand of hair was out of place. Who is your daughter? she was about to ask, but the woman was already talking again. 'Soon you will be with me, with us. We come from far off places to be together here. I'm waiting,' she said, and walked on.

Shocked, Raveena looked back at the woman. Out of the darkness in front of her she heard Sandy's call to hurry up or they would get late. 'I'm coming!' Raveena called out, and turned back again to look at the woman. But there was no one on the straight stretch of road in front of her. Trembling, Raveena forced herself to take a few steps and then ran as fast as she could to her friends. Overtaking them, she continued to run, with her friends following her, shouting out her name. They reached their room gasping for breath.

'Gosh! Why were you running like that, Raveena? We were not *that* late!' Sandy said, leaning against the wall of the corridor, while Mini was opening the door of their room. It was Mini who first noticed her roommate's chalk-white face. Raveena was shaking and gasping for air. Horrified she gestured to Sandy to look at Raveena. Sandy too lost her colour as she saw the state their friend was in. 'Open the door, she is going to fall down,' she screamed at Mini.

For the next half hour both the worried girls took care of Raveena. They made her drink some water, put a cloth soaked with cool water on her face, and massaged her feet.

'You didn't see her, did you?' Raveena asked feebly.

'Don't talk, just rest. You ran too fast,' Sandy said stroking her hair, relieved that her friend seemed to be returning to normal.

'I don't want to rest. Please listen to me—Mini, I saw your mother,' Raveena said, turning to the girl, who stepped away from the bed abruptly and turned pale.

'What are you saying? I don't have a mother. She died many years ago.

'I know...I know...I met her the first day I came here. She told me that I would meet you.'

'Look, you don't know what you are saying. Didn't you hear what Mini said: she doesn't have a mother, her mother passed away.'

'Be quiet Sandy. I may not get another chance to speak to you. Remember I had told you that I was not well? That's true, I was unwell, but not physically. I...I...for many years I have had a premonition about my death. Not just a premonition, I saw *where* I would die. I used to have nightmares; sometimes I'd be so scared, I'd get fits, break everything in my room, hurt myself. When I came here first, the place seemed similar to the one I'd seen in my nightmares. And now I realise it is not just similar, but *exactly* the same. The trees, the ivy...the mist. Everything.'

Genuinely frightened, Sandy and Mini held each other's hands.

'I was brought here for this reason only. My father thought it would help me overcome my fear to be in a place that was like the one I saw in my mind.'

'Please Raveena, we don't understand what you are talking about. I think we should call Sister, she will bring a doctor,' interrupted a visibly shaken Sandy.

'I'm telling the truth, Sandy,' Raveena shook her head agitatedly. 'When I first saw you Mini, didn't I say that I had seen you before? It was not you but your mother. You resemble her.' There was a pause, neither of her roommates said anything. Both of them were trembling.

'It's okay... you both go for dinner. I'll be fine, I'm tired, I just want to sleep now,' Raveena said feebly, closing her eyes. There was nothing that could be done now.

Sandy and Mini hastily left the room. As the door closed behind them, Raveena opened her eyes and cried. 'Oh Daddy! If only you could have understood. In a way you brought me to the doorsteps of my death.'

The door opened.

'Not feeling well, young lady? Your roommates told me that you think you saw a ghost?' Sister Margaret asked.

Raveena stared back at the nun stonily. She wanted to scream with rage and hit her. Choking back her emotions, she closed her eyes again.

'I know about your nightmares and fits. Your father told me everything. This is all psychological, everything is in your head, it is for you to decide whether you want to live with these fears or not.'

Raveena slowly opened her eyes again. Startled, the Sister took a few steps back from the bed. There was so much hatred in them.

Leaving the room, she murmured, 'Rest, I will call the doctor.'

♦

'Where is she?' the doctor enquired looking back at the Sister who was standing behind him, outside the room. The bed was empty and there was no one in the room.

'But she was just here a few minutes back when I left to call you...'

A search party was quickly formed. Her body was found the next day, late in the afternoon. Visibility was zero in the morning because of a thick mist which had hindered the search operations. She was hanging from a thick branch of a deodar tree, with strands of ivy coiled around her neck. Her eyes were wide open, staring into vacant space.

The Bhootwallahs

'So you want to hear the story...' she said, looking at me so intently that it made me a little nervous. 'Yes, yes. I was told it concerned a relative of yours. Your father I think,'

'Father! I don't even remember who my father was!' she blurted. 'It was my father-in-law. But why? What will it change? You youngsters don't believe in all this, no?'

My mind was racing. If I said no, would she tell me about her father-in-law? Weighing the pros and cons, I said, 'Well, I believe. Sometimes.'

'No,' she shook her head. 'You aren't sure. It's written in your eyes. Okay, tell me, are you scared of them?'

I was getting impatient. Why was she asking me all these questions? I was supposed to be the one doing all the asking, not she! 'Look Ammaji. I don't know what to say. If I'm scared or not is of no significance, I just wanted to ask you if the story was true,' I said, adding in case it helped, 'I am researching, you know. Like they do in colleges.'

'You young people!' she said scornfully. 'You think you can explain everything that crosses your path? Just like that?' she gesticulated angrily. 'What do you know about life? And who are you to decide what is true or not?' she nearly shouted.

Helplessly I stared at her. She looked furious. It was my fault, I thought: I shouldn't have been so direct and matter-of-fact. After all, we were stepping into delicate and personal territory.

'Ammaji, please don't take it this way. I am sorry if I have disturbed you, but believe me I didn't mean to,' I said cajolingly.

The old woman looked unmoved. Her gaze had shifted: she was now looking past me at the wide expanse behind my back. Was she dismissing me? Worried, I moved forward, my mind working furiously, wondering what I could say to pacify her. I could not let the entire trip go to waste. The last two days had been hectic. Locating her had been anything but easy. A two-hour journey by bus had brought me from Shimla to Theog, a small town on the Hindustan-Tibet Road. It took another hour for me to find a guide who would take me to her village. A good lot of persuasion and a Rs 50 note had convinced a young boy of about twelve to accompany me on the two-hour trek. It was sheer luck that, hardly had we walked a kilometre, than the boy suddenly stopped, pointed ahead excitedly and said, 'There she is, she must be coming to town. Now you go talk to her. I am going.' Relieved at having been saved the hike, I had walked up to the old woman, who was sitting comfortably, leaning against the thick trunk of a spruce tree.

And now I had spoilt it all with my impatience. I was about to say something when I heard her sigh. 'We are not like you. We never question our faith. Either it's there or not there. We don't need to have something proved before we believe it.' I nodded. Encouraged, she went on. 'What you are asking about is something that happened many years back. I don't understand what you will gain from hearing about it, but it meant a lot to me. It changed my life. Today, I believe life is very short; but life after death is a very long period. A period of silence. Long, long silence. And that is precisely why you are desperate to have your presence felt,' she said, her gaze wandering to the faraway woods.

I waited for her to resume her story. She finally turned her face to me: 'Has anyone ever thought about how lonely they feel who were once with their loved ones? They can't even talk to their own people—the people they left behind, their loved ones, their family, friends. Because whatever the circumstances, they're feared, shunned.'

I could see the sadness in her eyes. 'It's not their fault that they died,' she was saying. 'And what is death? It's only their bodies that have gone. Their spirits, their souls are alive, they are the same people who were once loved by the living. Why can't the living understand this?'

I could see her almost trembling with emotion. The thick branches of the spruce trees under which we sat stirred and swayed, as if in agreement with her.

◆

Many years back, fifty, maybe sixty, she wasn't sure, she had been married off. She could not have been more than twelve; she had almost no memories of her parents who had died when she was a child. She had been brought up by her uncle, her mother's brother.

Lato's in-laws included her two brothers-in-law, two sisters-in-law and her father-in-law. Her husband, Karam Singh, was the eldest son. She was welcomed warmly into the family; it was they who gave her the name Lato, out of affection.

In the beginning, it did not occur to her that there was something very odd about her husband's family. Very few people visited them or interacted with them. Both her sisters-in-law, who were of marriageable age, had failed to find any matches. They eventually died spinsters. Even her brothers-in-law did not get married though they were known to have relationships with women from the surrounding villages.

However, as time went by, she was able to pick up from what people around her said, that her new family were supposedly able to talk to spirits and ghosts. In fact, they were apparently friends with the spirits, listening to their woes, their joys and stories of life after death. It was her neighbour's little daughter who had told her that her family was known as the Bhootwallahs.

She ignored the rumours although she had heard strange noises coming from her father-in-law's room every evening. Since other family members seemed unconcerned about the noises, she ignored them too.

As the months rolled by, she became close to her father-in-law, and he eventually told her how her mother-in-law had died. It had been terror, sheer terror that had killed her. Her brother's ghost, she claimed, was playing pranks on her. He had died recently and she had not been by his side at that time. She said that his ghost troubled her, making his presence felt in every little corner of the house. Then one day he came in his human form, scaring her literally to death. She had a heart attack

Lato's father-in-law had been in the same room when the ghost had appeared that last time. However, instead of getting scared, he had been intrigued. He wanted to know more about life after death. Even as his wife lay dead, he tried to communicate with the ghost.

Later he developed the ability to see these spirits, or 'people who have left the earth' as he would call them. Every day, at about seven in the evening, he would lock himself up in his room. Sounds of loud laughter, crying, screaming, and howling would come out of the room. But it never scared anyone in the family. Sometimes the noises were a nuisance, disturbing their sleep, but never did anyone in the family fear anything. It had become a routine for them, and even if they felt curious about something, they kept it to themselves: Lato's father-in-law would never discuss what went on in the room with anyone else.

Some villagers said he performed black magic. Lato didn't believe that. What the villagers could never understand, and thus envied, was her father-in-law's amazing health. He finally died at the age of ninety-six. Some people said he had committed suicide, and some said his ghost friends had helped him do it.

She however had become part of his secret life. Twenty years after their marriage, her husband had died in an accident. He had fallen off a cliff one rainy night. He had been a gentle, loving husband and his death left her grieving for many months. One night, she woke up feeling thirsty. She went to the kitchen for a glass of water. As she stood there drinking the water, she heard someone talking inside her father-in-law's locked room. A few seconds later, she recognised the voice. It was her dead husband talking! She pounded on the door, pleading with her father-in-law to let her in as she too wanted to talk to her husband. She didn't know how long she stood outside, begging her father-in-law to open the door. Finally, she fell down exhausted. Her sister-in-law helped her to her room where Lato remained in a delirium for nearly three days. Her father-in-law didn't even come to see her once.

And then, exactly a week later, he came to her room and gestured for his daughters to leave them alone. Then he asked Lato to follow him. Though very weak, Lato eagerly followed him to his room. The door closed behind them, and from that moment, her life changed.

Over time he slowly taught her the art of talking to ghosts. She too could now enjoy the company of the loved ones who had 'left'. She met her mother-in-law for the first time. She chatted with her husband for hours. She understood that, like living human beings, spirits too wanted to be loved, to share their likes, dislikes and fears. They still possessed their personality traits: some were reserved, others were jovial, some naughty and impulsive, some clever and cunning...

◆

The old lady abruptly stopped talking. I cannot say I wasn't shaken. In fact, I was terribly scared and it was written all over my face. I felt cold and for a few moments could not look at her. Nor could I utter a single word. I'd only heard that her father-in-law had spoken with ghosts. No one had mentioned her! Had I known, I would never have come to see her alone.

'So child, I can see that you are also scared like the others,' I heard her say. I looked up. She was laughing. 'This is why I don't talk about it to anyone. No one understands. You are all the same,' she said slowly, shaking her head.

I looked down again, my mind in a whirl. I felt a movement, which made me turn towards her. She was getting up. Instinctively, I caught hold of her arm lest she should lose her balance.

'It's fine, I may be old but I can handle myself. Okay, now I am off to my village,' she said.

I was surprised. 'Weren't you going to Theog or somewhere else?' I asked her. Why else would she have been on the road?

She turned and looked at me. There was something about her gaze. I felt a strange chill down my spine.

'No, I came to meet you. My husband told me three nights back that you were trying to locate me. He said I should ensure you don't tire yourself walking all the distance to get to me. That I should cover some distance myself too.'

I stared at her. Fear. Disbelief.

'You are from a town, it would have been very inconvenient for you to walk on these rocky, narrow paths. Now go, write anything you want to. You said it is research. Go, write the report.'

And she turned and walked away.

The Sanjauli Fruit Seller

'In all Rs 5,' the vegetable seller told Atal, and then, turning to the man standing next to him, said, 'and yours Rs 4.50.'

'Add some dhania and hari mirch. That's the main reason I buy vegetable from you,' the man said.

Atal looked at the shopkeeper expectantly, hoping he would put some in his bag too.

'Good! Put some in his bag too, after all he has also bought from you,' his unknown companion said, pointing towards Atal.

'Thank you,' Atal murmured both to his companion and the vegetable seller.

'Are you from here? I mean Shimla?'

'No. I am from Ahmedabad. My sister has been

living here since she got married,' Atal replied. 'You must be from Shimla.'

'Yes, I work in the Accountant General's office. Are you here on holiday?' his companion asked as they climbed up towards the Lower Bazaar.

'Well, not exactly. It's been a month since I came here on doctor's advice. In fact, today is the first day I have come out.'

His companion stopped abruptly, causing the woman and small child behind them to nearly collide with him in the buzzing bazaar. Startled, Atal looked at him enquiringly.

'You look healthy to me... What has the doctor diagnosed?' his companion asked, beginning to walk again.

Atal was embarrassed. These paharis! They ask such personal questions! He didn't even know the man's name. Besides, he was in no mood to discuss his illness.

His companion, unaware of the discomfiture he had caused Atal, went on, 'Do you know Shimla was used as a sanatorium by the British?'

'Was it? I had no idea,' Atal said, relieved that the man was not insisting on being told what ailed him.

'Yes. The place was first selected for rejuvenating invalids or those Britishers who could not cope with the hot sultry weather of Calcutta. Gradually houses were built and later the Viceroy decided to shift the summer capital of the Raj here.'

'That's interesting,' said Atal.

'The Viceroys and Commander-in-Chiefs must have thought that it would be better to shift the capital to Shimla in summers as most of their officers were already here on "sick leave" or for holidays,' his companion chuckled, and then asked suddenly, 'Where does your sister reside?'

'At Sanjauli.'

For the second time his companion stopped abruptly. This time, a man did bump into him in the overcrowded Lower Bazaar.

'Why are you still here? Hurry up or you will miss the last bus to Sanjauli,' he said urgently.

'Oh I know, but I am not going by bus. I will walk back. I have to buy some groceries from a shop up ahead. Don't worry, my sister explained the directions to me,' said Atal, trying to calm his companion down.

'Okay, but you must hurry!' the man said looking worried. By this time they had reached a crossing from where Atal had to head in a different direction. He bid his companion goodbye and had hardly walked a few feet when he heard the man's unmistakable booming voice: 'Don't get late! The Snowdon-Sanjauli road is deserted at this time.' Surprised, Atal turned to ask what he meant by that, but the man had disappeared amongst the moving crowd.

Atal first stopped at a shop to buy his groceries and then decided to go to Minerva Bookstore to buy a book about Shimla's history. His companion had aroused his interest in Shimla's past.

'When does the Minerva Bookstore close, the one on the Mall?' he asked the shopkeeper.

'It might be closed by now, it is nearly 8.30 PM. Maybe if you hurry you will be lucky,' the shopkeeper replied.

He reached the bookstall just in time; the salesmen were about to leave and half the shutters were already down.

'Excuse me, I want to buy a book,' he said to the first person he saw at the counter.

'Which one?' the man asked politely.

Some minutes later Atal walked to Baljees Restaurant for a cup of coffee. He liked the cosy atmosphere in the restaurant; he felt comfortable enough to spend time there, browsing through his new book. Absorbed in the history of the town, he barely noticed the hours go by. When he called the waiter to order his fourth cup of coffee he was told the restaurant was closing for the night.

'Sorry, sir. But it's nearly 11 o' clock. Can I bring you your bill?' the waiter asked.

Atal stared at the waiter. Eleven already! Where had the time gone? He paid the bill, tucked the voluminous book under his armpit and stood up to leave.

'Which hotel are you staying in, sir?' the beaming waiter asked, as he picked up the bill along with the tip.

'Oh, I am not staying in a hotel. I am staying in Sanjauli with...' Atal stopped when he saw the look on the waiter's face.

'What is it? Did I say something wrong?' he asked anxiously.

'It's very late sir. How will you go to Sanjauli?'

'It's just a half hour walk from here, isn't it?' Atal said, taken aback by the waiter's reaction.

'You are not a local, that's why you haven't heard about the road.'

'Heard what?'

'Nothing, nothing...' the waiter said quickly, feeling that the outsider would think him a fool. 'But, you better hurry. If you find some other person going that way, accompany him. It is better to be two than one,' the waiter said cryptically before disappearing into the pantry.

Baffled, Atal left the restaurant. He wondered what was wrong with the Sanjauli Road that the two people he had spoken to had reacted thus. He had been for short walks on it a couple of times in the morning, and had enjoyed the shady, quiet road.

The cool crisp night air ruffled his hair as he climbed the steps adjoining the Municipal Corporation building near the Police Reporting Room on to the

Ridge. Enjoying the weather, and feeling happy that he was out and healthy once again, he walked briskly, whistling softly. Just as he passed Snowdon Hospital he heard the screams of a woman. Someone must have died, he thought. Immediately, as if someone had thrown cold water on him, his mood changed. Death is so frightening, he thought. Imagine losing someone dear to you. How final it all was. *God give them strength*, he prayed as he walked on.

It struck Atal odd that he had not met anyone after he had left the restaurant. His eyes scanned the darkness to see if there was anyone ahead. Apart from the silhouettes of the tall conifer and oak trees that lined both sides of the road, he could see nothing. Suddenly, for no apparent reason, a cold fear gripped him.

'This is ridiculous, in twenty minutes I am going to reach Sanjauli,' he said aloud. An uneasy feeling was overpowering him. There is nothing to be scared of, he reassured himself. But the fear did not pass. He remembered the waiter's face at Baljees. Atal still didn't understand what he had meant, but there was something about the waiter's behaviour that troubled him now. He could feel the sweat in both his palms as he tightly clutched his bags.

Suddenly, something overcame him when he reached the water bauri. His legs became heavy as lead. He had to muster all his strength to make them move. The atmosphere seemed to take on an eerie feel. Petrified, he did not notice the man in white until he was just a few steps away. At the same moment, he felt as if someone had passed by him and was now behind him. He looked around quickly but could not see anyone. He panicked. He turned in front. No one there either. Where had the man in white gone? Or were there two men? Wanting to scream he forced himself to walk on. Finally he passed the bauri. Almost immediately, the heaviness in his legs vanished just as suddenly as it had come.

I was just getting paranoid, he told himself and tried to smile, but failed. A few minutes later he heard voices ahead of him. He started praying and muttering 'om, om, om'. The fear that had subsided gripped his whole being again.

The voices were becoming louder and clearer. As he turned the next curve in the road, he could see two figures. 'Oh God! Please help me,' he moaned.

'Excuse me, how far is the Mall from here?' enquired a young voice.

Atal almost laughed out loud with relief. They were just youngsters! 'It'll take you about twenty minutes,' he replied.

'Twenty minutes?' the boy said, turning to his companion, 'You said we should reach in another five minutes!'

'Oh, shut up! It's nothing, can't you walk this little...' their voices faded as Atal moved on ahead, mocking himself for his fears.

'Oranges. Sweet oranges.' Atal turned. The voice had come from the rain shelter. Peering into the darkness, he approached the sitting figure. 'What? Are you selling oranges? Now?' he asked as he stopped near the fruit seller.

'Anyway, it's a relief to see you. I will take a dozen. How much?' Atal asked as he squatted to choose the best fruits. It was then that he saw the man's hands. They were lying lifeless on both sides of the tokra: they were blackish and hairy...and were turned inwards!

Atal shuddered. He stumbled backwards, picked himself up and ran away from the shelter. The tinkling of a bicycle bell ahead slowed him down and he cried, 'Stop, stop! Don't go ahead. There is a man...a man selling oranges. He has different kinds of hands...Please don't go there,' he wailed, not quite knowing what he was saying. He could feel the sweat pouring down his back as he clutched the handle of the bicycle.

'Were his hands like this?' the calm voice penetrated his disoriented mind. Atal stared down at the bicycle handle that he was holding. Right next to his, was a pair of the same grotesque hands.

He slumped down unconscious on the spot.

Bhoot Bangla

If I described the house to you, it would seem like an ordinary, run-of-the-mill house. Single storey, with a terrace and a chimney. And yet, if you were standing at the gates, looking at the structure, an involuntary chill would creep down your spine. The broken glass in the windows, the empty fish pond in front of the house, the two trees in the courtyard that have been leafless since anyone can remember...it is all these and more. It is difficult not to feel as though you were being warned to stay away by the very atmosphere.

♦

'Lucky Sinhas,' Rakesh said.

'Yes, Rs 3 crore for the Bhoot Bangla! Unbelievable!' Ajay responded.

'Modernisation and progress are inimical to ghosts. Commercial prospects have no value for rumours, superstitions and tales of the supernatural,' Rakesh said softly.

Rakesh—of medium height and a thin frame—was philosophical, intelligent and shrewd. He had very sharp eyes—large, fiery, penetrating. He was clean shaven with a thick, untidy mop of hair that was prematurely greying. Ajay was about six-feet-tall; his round face almost always cheerful.

The childhood friends gazed at the Bhoot Bangla. The building and the surrounding land had been acquired recently to construct a residential colony. They were sitting at pathar, a vantage point in the Navbahar forest which offered a panoramic view of Sanjauli. They had come there after a gap of several years, having left Shimla for work soon after college. Now, as they looked at the landscape around them, they realised that Sanjauli had changed for the worse.

'Look at the number of houses, how they have mushroomed. They're like matchboxes precariously placed one on top of the other,' Rakesh said.

Ajay nodded in agreement.

'What are you thinking about?' asked Rakesh.

'How many years ago was that? Ten?'

'No yaar, we were in second year. 1986.'

'My God! Unbelievable.'

'Look, there is someone at the Bhoot Bangla near the bauri,' Ajay said excitedly and then asked, 'Do you think of that night?'

'Many times,' Rakesh murmured.

◆

They had decided to go on a trekking trip to Junga, about thirty kilometres from Sanjauli. There had been five of them: Rakesh, Ajay, Vipul, Chinnu and Hutashan. It was a long trek, and they had prepared well: they were carrying tents, sleeping bags, a stove, cooker, plates, food. They had planned the four-day trek meticulously, but somehow everything went wrong.

The friends set out for the trek in the middle of November. On the second day they reached Junga in high spirits. Everything was going according to plan, and they were having a great time. Tired but excited and not yet worn out they began their return journey on the third day.

Junga, a large village, is at a lower elevation than Shimla, so they knew that the journey back to their homes would involve steep climbs, would be tougher and take them more time. However their progress was slow, and it was quite late when they reached the camping site for the day. Hurriedly they made Maggie noodles and soup which they ate with buttered bread under the moonlight. All of them were tired by now, and no one had the energy to pitch the tents, so they slept under the open star-studded sky.

The next morning, all of them were suffering from cramps, headache and tiredness. Rakesh was the only one who had some energy to cook breakfast. They still had to cover over fifteen kilometres to reach their homes. Of this, two kilometres were a steep ascent.

Vipul was exhausted, and the trek ahead seemed torturous to him. He repeatedly suggested that they spend one more day there resting, but no one listened to him.

'Come on buddy, don't look so pathetic. Where has all the enthusiasm for trekking and adventures disappeared?' Ajay said, laughingly.

With a lot of grumbling from Vipul and determination from the others, they set off. Every fifteen minutes Vipul would have to sit to rest his tired body. His rucksack was being carried in turn by the others, as he was in no position to carry it himself.

At about 3 o' clock in the afternoon they rested for an hour to eat and rejuvenate their energies.

'I don't think I can make it!' Vipul said, dejectedly.

'You can! We all will. We have taken the short cut, which means just about four hours to reach home from here. Except the last 800 metres, the rest is an easy walk,' Rakesh said reassuringly.

'Are you mad? 800 metres! I am not even able to walk, how will I climb? Why did you change the route?' Vipul said indignantly, worry written all over his face.

'Because, Fatso, this is a shortcut and we will reach our houses directly from here,' said Chinnu.

'Really? And how in hell are we going to climb that mountain in the dark?' Vipul returned morosely. There was silence. He was right. It was going to be dark soon and it would be difficult to find their way in unknown territory.

Rakesh broke the uneasy silence, 'Come on! Let's move.'

For more than three hours they trudged on. Energy was low. Two of them—Hutashan and Ajay—had hurt themselves while groping in the dark. Three torch batteries had been exhausted. On top of all this, it had started drizzling.

'Hey, is that a house?' Ajay asked. Rakesh looked in the direction Ajay was pointing at and saw the silhouette of a house. The moon too had disappeared into the clouds and there was darkness all around. Suddenly the slight drizzle changed to a heavy downpour and the boys helplessly stood where they were, the rain soaking them.

'Why did this have to happen with us?' moaned Chinnu.

'Look, I am sure there is a house. There is no light though. The people who live there must have gone out somewhere. But there must be a veranda or some other shelter. Let's go,' Ajay said.

'How much more time will it take?' asked Vipul.

'At least twenty minutes... Somehow, I don't feel comfortable going there. It's so lonely,' Rakesh said slowly.

'I am very much liking the idea! Come on, we will freeze to death if we don't decide soon!' moaned Chinnu.

'Chinnu is right. We've come across a shelter, we can't ignore it. Only a fool would do that. Let's move guys,' Hutashan said, giving a push to Vipul who was in front of him.

'Ouch! What's that?' Vipul screamed. Something sharp was poking him below his knees.

'There's a wire here, the place is fenced. I hope there are no dogs here,' muttered Chinnu.

'I know where we are,' Ajay said loudly.

'Good. I have been racking my brain to figure that out. Where are we?' asked Rakesh.

'At Bhoot Bangla,' Ajay said dramatically.

The statement was met with an ominous silence. The rain was pelting down heavily on them. Their rucksacks had become heavy as lead, and their fingers and toes were numb with cold.

Though just a forty-five minute walk from their locality, they had never visited the place. Without a word to each other they moved towards the house. They were too tired to think about ghosts.

It took them another ten minutes after crossing the fence to reach the house. Rakesh had a narrow escape: he slipped and, had it not been for Ajay who managed to catch hold of him in time, he would have fallen into the gorge below, seriously injuring himself, if not worse.

When the group shone their torch around, the place looked more eerie than comfortable. After prowling around for some time they found a window latch open.

'Let's not investigate further but settle down in the room,' Rakesh said.

'This is the last torch we have got. At least let us find some logs first, dry ones. I'm shivering,' Vipul said.

'You should thank your stars that we have found shelter. We won't get any dry wood here. Let's all huddle together in a corner,' Chinnu said. And that is what they did.

'Why is this house called Bhoot Bangla?' Vipul asked after some time.

'God knows. I have heard it being called Bhoot Bangla for so long that I never took the trouble of asking anyone why it got that name,' said Ajay.

'It looks quite normal to me,' said Chinnu tentatively. No one replied.

'What's wrong? Are you people scared?' he spoke again.

'Shut up! Let's change the topic,' Hutashan said a little aggressively.

'Are there any biscuits left?' asked Vipul.

Ajay silently passed the last biscuit packet. For the next three hours the boys talked about everything except ghosts. Slowly, they all fell asleep.

◆

Rakesh opened his eyes. Bright sunlight hit him hard and he closed his eyes again instantly. There was something wrong. A few seconds later he opened them again and looked around.

'What the hell...' he said aloud. How could this be? The other four were also sprawled around on the ground near the red pond! Their rucksacks, which they had been using in the room as pillows, were strewn in the veranda and their belongings were littered all over the compound. The wrapper of the last biscuit packet was fluttering on top of one of the rucksacks.

Despite the hot sun he felt a chill. He got up quickly, shouting at the other four to wake up.

The rest was a blur. It was only when they were some distance away from the house that they stopped to catch their breath to try and figure out what had happened.

◆

Later, they came to know the story behind the Bhoot Bangla. The current owner, Mr Sinha, had bought the property from a Muslim family in 1947 at the time of Partition. Their eldest daughter was of a religious disposition and used to recite her prayers at a place that happened to be near the grave of a pir in the compound of the house. Apparently this must have angered the pir. No one knew what happened exactly, but the girl went mad. Her family kept her locked in a closed room in the house, where she eventually died. After her death her family moved out of the house.

Thereafter, many people had heard screams, howls and high-pitched laughter from the house at night. And it came to be called Bhoot Bangla.

The boys were also told that whoever slept in the house found themselves thrown out into the compound!

The Road to Lovers' Paradise

'Lovers' Paradise—how does the name sound madam?' Aakash teased his newly-wedded wife. Geetanjali blushed and he laughed, touching her lightly on her arm. She immediately withdrew, looking at him shyly. Shaking her head she indicated the presence of the driver with her eyes. He laughed again.

Aakash turned to look out of the window at the scenery. Shimla 7 km, the milestone read as the van sped on. He had seen hoardings advertising Hotel Lovers' Paradise twice.

An accountant in a private company at Chandigarh, he and Geetanjali had been married just two days back. He had been given only seven days' leave for the wedding. The couple had been undecided between Shimla and Kullu for their honeymoon. Finally his mother had suggested Shimla. It was only a three-hour journey, and as he had only four days, he could spend them leisurely. Also, Geetanjali had never been to Shimla before.

Theirs had been an arranged marriage. During their eight-month engagement period they had communicated through letters. Geetanjali was an introvert and it was only when the marriage date came closer, did her letters become more forthcoming and affectionate.

'Is that Shimla?' Geetanjali asked excitedly. Aakash turned and stared at the ridge and slopes that resembled a concrete jungle.

'Yes. It has changed a lot, it seems to have become very congested now,' he said. 'I never thought it would become like this,' he added.

'Neither did I.'

'What do you mean,' he said, turning to her.

'It's so different from what I had thought it would be. These slopes are covered by houses. I mean, there are some trees, but it is not like Dalhousie,' she said.

'Have you been to Dalhousie?' he asked.

'Yes, with Papa, about two years ago after I finished my graduation,' she said shyly.

'We have reached sahib. Have you booked in some hotel?' the driver interrupted.

'Take us to Lovers' Paradise,' Aakash said without thinking.

'The hotel is on a restricted road, taxis are not allowed. I will take you till Lady Reading Hospital, from there it's just a fifteen-minute walk,' the driver said.

Aakash nodded and then looked at his bride. She was busy combing her hair and tying it back in a knot at the nape of her neck.

'Oh, my God!' she suddenly screamed, cringing away from the open window of the van.

'Don't worry, they are coolies, Kashmiri Khans,' the driver said.

'But why are they running around the van? They will hurt themselves. What do they want?' she asked.

'Ignore them, they are looking for customers. It's always like this. This place is called Victory Tunnel; tourists from buses get down here and then the Khans take over, leading them to hotels. This is how they earn their livelihood,' Aakash explained, holding his wife close.

'You have to be very careful of them sahib, they also fleece tourists. There is a strong nexus between them, the transporters and hoteliers,' warned the driver. 'Here we are. Lovers' Paradise is quite near, a small steep climb. You do not have much luggage, but if you need a coolie you will get one at the shop ahead,' he added.

It took them more than fifteen minutes to reach the hotel. Lovers' Paradise was well marked; a bridle path set in a thick conifer forest led to it.

Geetanjali began to feel sick as soon as she started to climb the path. In the beginning she felt an acute tiredness, and then she started shivering involuntarily.

'Are you feeling cold?' Aakash asked.

'I don't know, it's a very...strange feeling,' she said weakly. She had wanted to say eerie, but had checked herself.

The feeling passed when they reached the hotel. Both of them were relieved to get a room, and despite the dismal entrance, the hotel, with its big glass windows, gave a panoramic view of Shimla and its surrounding peaks. Geetanjali was delighted with the posh deluxe room. The view from the window was superb, it made her feel as if they were on top of the world!

'I am so glad that you chose this hotel,' she said happily, clapping her hands like a child. Amused by her child-like happiness, Aakash opened his arms for her to come and join him on the sofa settee. With slow steps she moved towards him. He made her sit on his lap.

'You weren't so excited before, while we were coming up to the hotel; you felt cold and funny,' he said huskily, stroking her head lightly.

She did not reply, but she did not move away. There had been something there: she had felt a chill.

It was as if someone was stopping her from entering his or her domain. She could not understand the feeling herself, and she dared not try to explain it to Aakash. He might think that she was some superstitious village girl who believed in these illogical things.

'Maybe we should bathe and then go out to see the town,' she said hesitantly.

'Hmm. You are right, it is just 3 o' clock. You go first,' he said. 'I will unpack in the meanwhile. What will you wear?'

'Anything.'

'Fine, you carry on, I will hand you your clothes in a few minutes,' he said.

She opened the bathroom door. It was quite spacious with nice blue tiling. She opened the hot water tap and after about two mugs of cold water, hot water started coming out

'Hey Geet, is this blue suit okay?' Aakash called from the room. The bucket was nearly full. Closing the tap, she opened the bathroom door.

'The blue suit will be fine, thanks,' she said taking it from him.

When Geetanjali poured the first mug of water over her body, she literally jumped, letting out an involuntary scream. The water was as cold as ice. Shivering, she quickly rubbed herself with a towel and put on her clothes.

'So soon! There are a lot of things that we need to know about each other, you really are quick lady!'

'I...er...are you also going to have a bath?'

'Yes, of course.'

'I think the water is cold, wait for sometime, let it heat up,' she said shakily.

'Is the geyser on?'

'Yes.'

Aakash nodded as he took out his shaving kit and the clothes that he wanted to change into.

Geetanjali moved towards the glass window hugging herself tight, trying to understand what had happened. She could still feel the chill in her bones, and yet she could have sworn the water had been hot when she was filling the bucket.

'Geet, the water is very hot. I'm switching off the geyser,' Aakash shouted from the bathroom. Unnerved she went up to the bathroom door.

'Is it hot?'

'Of course silly. You yourself have filled the bucket. You must not have checked properly,' he said while shaving.

Slowly she moved towards the bucket and dipped her hand. Yes, it was hot! How could it be? What was happening? She felt cold fear grip her heart.

'Are you not feeling well Geet?' Aakash asked worried. He was watching his wife; her face had gone white, her right hand, still resting on the rim of the bucket, was trembling. Aakash put his shaving brush on the washbasin and caught hold of his wife's hand.

'Geet,' he said moving her towards the bedroom. 'Come, lie down. You better rest. If you want, we will not go out today,' he said gently.

'No, no, it's fine, you have your bath. I will rest for sometime. Maybe it's the journey or the exertion of the last two days,' she said lamely.

'Are you sure?' he asked, touching her forehead gently.

'Yes. Please, we will go to the market too. I think I will feel better,' she said smiling.

When he went into the bathroom she got up from the bed and started pacing in the room. She was not mistaken: first the sensation when approaching the hotel, then the water in the bathroom. 'I must be careful,' she thought. 'I can't take the risk of telling him that there is a ghost here, he won't believe me. Oh God! What should I do?' she murmured.

Geetanjali possessed the ability to sense the presence of a wandering spirit. Her maternal aunt, who had helped her understand this special power, used to take her to houses in the village to find out whether a spirit was present or not. The symptoms included shivering, uneasiness and a basic intuition that something was present. This power had never bothered Geetanjali before. But now she felt confused. She was not sure how Aakash would react to it.

The bathroom door opened and Aakash came out whistling.

'Feeling better?'

'Yes, should we go?'

'You really are in a hurry! Let me at least wear my shoes,' he said laughing.

Geetanjali tidied the room while he got ready. A few minutes later she went into the bathroom to sort out their toiletries. Immediately the queer sensation overtook her; the violent shivering returned, making her gasp.

'I am ready Geet, let's move,' Aakash said. Mustering all her strength, she walked out of the bathroom, closing the door behind her firmly.

For the next five hours, the couple had a good time. They walked to the Indian Institute of Advanced Studies, loitered on the Mall and the Ridge, and shopped at the Himachal Emporium. They dined at Plaza Restaurant, a chance finding a few steps down from the Mall.

'One last round,' Aakash said as they left the restaurant.

'Isn't it late?'

'Not at all! Moreover, our hotel is quite near. But are you tired? I completely forgot about your illness back at the hotel.'

'I'm fine now, just a little tired. We must have walked more than ten kilometres today!' she said, and then added thoughtfully, 'I don't know what happened there.' The fear returned. She wanted to say that there was a spirit, and it was waiting for them, but she didn't have the courage.

'Here we are! The last stretch to the Paradise,' Aakash said as they stepped on the bridle path to their hotel.

'It's very dark,' she said, her mouth dry with fear

'Don't worry, we'll find our way.'

For a minute, they walked hand-in-hand silently, and then he stopped.

'Just smell the fragrance of the pine, the wet earth. This is what you can't get in cities,' he said.

Geetanjali's heart was hammering. A chill seeping into her body, she felt an unknown terror clutch her whole being. Why did he have to stop? she silently moaned.

Unaware of what his wife was going through, Aakash leaned on the railing, pulling her into his arms. As she adjusted her head on his shoulder, the howling started. At first, it was soft, but then it gradually picked up and turned into fearsome laughter. It made her cringe. She tried to shut out the sound, but it went on, becoming louder, coming closer. She hadn't realised that she was clutching Aakash's arm tight until he gave out a cry, 'Ouch! You're hurting me Geet!' he said. She heard him as if he was speaking from far off. The screams, the laughter, the howling had penetrated her whole sensory system.

And then she saw the hazy figure of a woman some fifty metres ahead, amidst the trees. The woman stood there in the grove for a few seconds, and then moved slowly away, disappearing into the woods.

She had seen a spirit for the first time in her life, and, despite her fear, she wanted to talk to her. What did she want? Why was she still wandering in this life?

Geetanjali jerked her head up. Aakash was talking and his voice was so clear. They were climbing the last steps leading into the hotel, his hand firmly gripping her elbow. When had they covered the distance? she wondered. Startled she looked back. There was nothing except for the darkness.

'Good evening Madam, Sir. How did you like Shimla?' the man at the reception desk said.

'I have been here several times, but it's my wife's first visit.'

Both the men looked at her, one affectionately and the other politely. She pulled herself up. She had to answer, say something, it was expected of her.

'It's a very lovely place,' she mumbled, just before she fainted.

For Aakash, the night was a torture. He did not sleep a wink. The doctor diagnosed tiredness and exhaustion. When Geetanjali regained consciousness she went into a delirium. She was mumbling and fretting and her body temperature had risen to 105° C.

The hotel staff was very helpful, regularly supplying cubes of ice to be placed on her forehead to lower her fever.

In the morning the couple left for PGI Hospital at Chandigarh and so their honeymoon ended.

♦

The shopkeeper on the Mall opposite the bridle path stared at the departing couple. It always happens with the women, he thought. There had been a house on the land where the hotel now stood. The house had been his. He had to sell it cheaply because the women in his family refused to live there. They claimed that the ghost of an English woman wandered near the house, making unbearable noises in the surrounding thick deodar jungle.

Later, he had found out that during the Raj, there used to be a small graveyard in the area. His wife was sure that their house had been built on the grave of an unhappy memsahib. Finally the house had been demolished some years back to make way for the hotel.

Houses can be destroyed, graves can't.

The Ghost on the Railway Line

Amit looked with satisfaction at his table, empty except for a glass of water, a golden pen stand and a map of the Northern Railways. There was not one pending file on his table. Experience had taught him not to delay work if he wanted to avoid complications and tension.

'When will Mr Sharma come?' a man asked, peering from behind the half open door.

'I am the Station Master now,' Amit replied briskly. 'Mr Amitabh Sharma has been transferred to Lucknow.'

The man opened the door and entered. 'Namaskar sir. My name is Manoj Chauhan. I am a contractor. I'm sorry, I didn't know that Sharmaji had been transferred.'

'He left last week. Can I help you?' Amit asked politely.

'You belong to which place, sir?'

'Bangalore. Do sit down. Is it always so hot here? I thought the weather in Shimla would be cold.'

'No, but today the temperature is abnormally high. Have you shifted into the official accommodation?'

'No, not yet. Sharmaji has not yet taken his luggage. For the time being I am staying in the Railway Rest House,' he said, and then added, 'How can I help you?'

'I have an orchard at Kotgarh. I had brought a box of apples for Sharmaji, but as he has left, er, should I keep it in your room in the guest house?'

Amit didn't want any gifts from an unknown contractor. Moreover, he had brought them for his predecessor. Was it meant to be some kind of bribe? he wondered. He tried to refuse politely, but the contractor was insistent. 'Please sir, it is just a gift from Himachalis. I will not take no from you.'

Before Amit could say anything, he interrupted, 'Have you been around the town?'

'Well, not yet. I get free by 7 o' clock in the evening, and after that I just take a long walk, usually on the railway line towards Summer Hill.'

'Don't do that!' the contractor said abruptly.

'Why not?' Amit asked, taken aback.

'It's not safe.'

'Oh, it's all right. There is no train in the evening. Tunnel number 103 is dirty but—'

'—Forget about the dirtiness. You should not use the tunnels at night,' his guest said agitatedly. 'I better leave, I will put the box in your room. I hope you like the apples,' he said, getting up.

Amit stared at the closed door thoughtfully for some time and then got back to his work.

The fragrance of apples reached his nostrils as he entered the guest room later that evening. He opened the box, took out a large red apple and bit into it guiltily. While he devoured the juicy fruit, he decided that when the contractor came the next time he would pay for the apples. He had eaten two apples and had sat down to write a letter to his family when the peon walked in.

'Feeling hungry, sahib?' Pal Singh asked, as he placed a tray of food on the table.

'Not much, I had a couple of apples. You people are very lucky to have this fruit in abundance,' he said shutting the letter pad.

'You are right, sahib,' the peon said, and left the officer to eat his food in privacy.

'I have had enough Pal Singh, take the tray away,' Amit called.

'Yes sahib. Should I bring your tea now?'

'No, I will go for my walk first. I'll have my tea when I get back,' he said.

'A walk? Now? It is very late sahib...forget the walk for today.'

'Why? It's just 9 o' clock. In cities we are out till midnight,' Amit said from the bathroom as he washed his hands. When he returned to the room, Pal Singh was still there with the plate in his hand.

'What is it?' he asked.

'I am a small man sahib, you are a big officer. Please don't mind my saying, but here no one goes for walks so late. It is not safe.'

'What are you talking about? Are there dacoits here?' Amit asked, smiling.

Sensing that the sahib was in no mood to listen, Pal Singh decided to adopt a new approach. 'If you *have* to go, please don't follow the railway line through the tunnel. You can walk on the National Highway.'

Dismissing the peon with the assurance that he would be careful, Amit bolted his room from outside and walked towards the railway line.

What are they scared about? he wondered. He knew the crime rate in Himachal was negligible; the people were a satisfied lot, peace-loving, honest and sincere. Why should there be any problem going for a walk at night?

He switched on his torch as he entered the tunnel. Immediately, he began to feel a little cold. He wrapped his overcoat tighter around him. It was dark inside, despite the torchlight, and he stumbled. Regaining his balance he stood there for a second, trying to decide whether to continue or return. He decided to move on.

After a few minutes he emerged out of the claustrophobic chill of the tunnel into the open, fresh air. Then, for no particular reason, Amit began to feel scared. As he looked around, his fear increased. The dense jungle and the dimly visible railway line stretching into infinity like a thick coil combined to create a sense of dread inside him. Could there be wild animals here? The contractor and Pal Singh must have been referring to wild animals when they said it was not safe, he thought. Amit tried to calm himself and turned to go back to the rest house.

As he looked at the tunnel, the black hole seemed intimidating, frightening. How was he going to go through it? He felt his legs trembling. What's wrong with you? Are you mad? Just now you came through this thing. There was nothing there and there is no other option but to go through it to reach the comfort of your room, he said loudly to himself. Without waiting for any other foolish idea to enter his mind, he walked into the black hole.

He could hear his heart hammering in his breast with every step he took. The darkness and the chill engulfed him. His mind stopped working. With leaden limbs he forced himself to move forward, continuously peering ahead to see how much further was the tunnel's opening. But he could make out nothing.

Within seconds, terror had overtaken him completely and he sat down helplessly. The torch fell from his hands and rolled away.

'God help me,' he sobbed. He had never experienced such fear in his life. And he didn't even know the reason for his fear.

'Are you all right?'

Startled, Amit looked up. A man was standing a few feet away from him. He could just make out the outline of the man's body; his face wasn't visible. For some reason, Amit got the feeling that he was tall, very tall. Then he lost control of himself as tears rolled down his cheeks, he didn't know whether he was crying in relief or in fear.

'I don't know what happened, it was all so sudden...the fear. It was as if I was waiting for something bad to happen!' he said lamely a minute later, when he had got control over himself.

'Get up, come with me. I will take you out of the tunnel,' the man said.

'I felt trapped: I got the feeling that I would never be able to get out of this darkness. There wouldn't be an opening and I would suffocate here only,' Amit said in a terrified voice, slowly getting up. 'How glad I am that you came along! I am the new Station Master here,' he said awkwardly, by way of introducing himself.

The man remained silent.

'I have lost my torch, it must be somewhere here,' Amit said, looking around vaguely.

'Leave it! Just follow me,' the voice snapped.

Startled by his tone, Amit did what he was told. In less than a minute he could make out the end of the tunnel.

'Thank God we have reached! How long were you in the tunnel? I mean, were you going somewhere...?' he said conversationally as relief flooded him.

'I just wander around here.'

Trying to decipher what the man meant, Amit stepped out of the tunnel into the fresh air. He looked around for his companion, but there was nobody. It was as if he had come out of the tunnel alone!

He had no idea how he reached his room that night. The next morning, when he asked Pal Singh about the tunnel, the peon told him that a few people had come across an Englishman's ghost in the tunnel. Amit had not seen the spirit's face, so he didn't know whether it was an Englishman or an Indian. But he had met him. There was no doubt about that. And for the next three years that he stayed in Shimla, he never went for walks in the night!

Enduring Love

Chhaya looked down silently from the balcony at the marriage preparations going on below. Final touches were being given to the entrance gate and porch. Only eight hours were left for the arrival of the baraat.

She stared blankly at the giggling girls—friends of her younger sister—who were blowing balloons downstairs. They looked funny, in an ugly way, with their cheeks bloated and their henna-dyed hands clutching the balloons. One of the girls saw Chhaya, and excitedly pointed her out to the others who all squealed. They looked uglier.

The previous evening all of them had had their hands decorated with henna. Chhaya had remained indifferent as her palms and feet had been adorned with designs of flowers and leaves. It struck her as odd that the green henna would eventually dye her hands red. Where did the green go? And from where did the red come? Wasn't it unnatural for a colour to lose its original hue and acquire a totally different shade?

The mehendi festivities went on till two in the morning, with every woman of the village aged between five and seventy-five singing, dancing and having their hands painted.

Chhaya felt removed from all the festivity. She had passed the night sitting with her feet and hands spread out in front of her so as not to smudge the henna. By morning, her body had been so numb, that when she put her feet down to stand up, a piercing pain had shot upwards. She would have fallen but for her father who caught her in time. A big man with a jolly nature, he helped her take the first painful steps.

'Take care of the bride, women, she is falling here and there. Treat her like a princess, wash her hands and feet in the room itself,' he said. 'You, there. Bring that bucket and mug,' he added, gesturing to her cousin who was plaiting Chhaya's grandmother's hair.

The gentle massage did bring life back to her limbs.

♦

'What are you thinking, child? This is the fate of all women. We are born and brought up in one house, and are sent to another when we grow up. In the beginning it feels as if we have no place of our own, but believe me, after some time, our husband's house becomes our real home,' her grandmother said as she joined Chhaya on the balcony.

Chhaya did not even turn her head, tears pricked her eyelids.

'Cry beta, cry, it makes you lighter. Like any other girl you have the right to cry when you leave your parent's home. These tears will release the tension,' the old woman said softly.

Chhaya opened her mouth to say something, anything, but nothing came out. She had bottled up her feelings for so long that now she felt helpless. Her fear, her dread and her nightmares were her own, not to be shared. She felt a headache coming on.

'Take the advice of this old woman, forget your past. You have no choice. You will leave us soon, nothing can change that, beta,' her grandmother added.

Chhaya's clasp on the balcony railing tightened; her spine felt stiff and her frail frame trembled. With an effort that required all her energy she said, 'I tried. No one believes me. I am still trying. My past is not yet buried, daadi. I am serious. I am not mad.' She turned, but her grandmother had already moved to the other corner of the room and was chatting with the women making garlands. She stared at her grandmother uncomprehendingly, and then helplessly. 'Why don't you help me daadi? No one listens to me,' she whispered.

The family had decided that the topic was never to be entertained, even if she spoke about it. No one was to let her talk about her past.

He will never allow me to marry someone else, she thought.

◆

She'd had a fairly normal childhood till the nightmares started when she was ten. Every time she had one, she could not sleep out of fear for days. Initially, her dreams did not make any sense; they were just a series of images. Sometimes she saw a young girl dressed in marriage finery. Always she saw the girl jumping in a black dark gorge. Chhaya felt that she was that girl although the face she saw in her dreams was not hers. Sometimes she saw a boy saying something that she could not decipher. Every time she had the dream she woke up sweating.

Slowly a picture began emerging and she knew that what she was seeing were not mere dreams, but visions that were revealing the horrific story of an earlier birth. She understood from her visions that she used to live in a large double-storey building in Tutu, a small village on the outskirts of Shimla. She studied at a school in Shimla, about seven kilometres from her home. It was while she was in school that she had fallen in love with him. He had left school in the fifth standard and worked as an assistant in a jewellery shop on the Mall. Eventually, they decided to elope, but before they could take the step her family got to know. She was thrashed and confined inside the house by her parents and brothers.

It was 1948, a year after India had gained independence. A few Britishers had decided to stay back in India. One such Briton, Mr Smith Lock, an old man whose one arm had been amputated, lived in a small bungalow near her house. He was popularly known as Angrez, being the only Caucasian in the locality. He not only helped her cope with her confinement, shame, guilt and anger, but also acted as a conduit between her and her lover. After about a month, her marriage was fixed to a rich businessman. When she was told about it, she jumped from the second storey of her house. She survived the fall, but fractured her legs, broke her wrist and had a minor head injury.

Her family members told their relatives that she had accidentally fallen, but they blamed her for shaming them in the locality. Her marriage was postponed by two months. The boy visited her every day at the Ripon Hospital where she was admitted, during the two hours that Angrez uncle looked after her. She cared for nothing, except his visits. She hoped that they would be able to go away together after she was discharged.

It was almost a month after the accident that her brothers arrived unexpectedly at the hospital and caught him there with her. Her brothers must have known about their rendezvous as they walked in holding an iron rod. Angrez uncle had left them alone half an hour back, so she was the only witness to his murder. Her younger brother hit him on the head with the iron rod till he collapsed on the floor. His last look and words were imprinted in her mind. As he slid down, he had said, 'She is mine, she will always be mine, no one else will marry her, I will not allow it, I will take care of this forever.'

She never saw Angrez uncle again. In fact, she never saw or heard anyone else again as she slid into a coma from which she never surfaced.

♦

Chhaya had begged her parents to take her to Tutu so that they could find out whether what she dreamt was true. When they reached the village, she instinctively went the house that she had lived in. There, they found out that her parents in her earlier birth had died more than a decade back. Her younger brother had recently lost his life in an accident, after having served a ten-year term in jail for murder. Her elder brother was now about sixty-five years old. When Chhaya's family explained why they were there, he turned away from her in pain and disgust. He cursed her for what she had done to the family and locked himself in his room, refusing to say anything more to her.

Forced now to accept what Chhaya had been saying, her family was traumatised. Then they simply stopped speaking about it. Although Chhaya's nightmares stopped, because she now knew the truth, she had a strong premonition that something horrific would happen when her marriage was fixed.

Even now, as her family ran around making sure everything was all right before the baraat arrived, Chhaya felt as though she were just waiting for something to happen. She knew that he would not allow the marriage: her belief was so strong that she had not even looked at her fiance's face on the engagement day. She had tried to explain to her family that it was wrong to carry on with the facade. First they had tried to reassure her that it was impossible for someone from a previous life to have any effect on her now, but as her protests continued, they had simply ignored her.

◆

'Chhaya, don't stand there beta. Hurry up and change into the yellow suit, the last and fifth ceremony of batana is to take place. The beautician has also arrived,' her mother said, putting her arm around Chhaya's shoulders.

Like a puppet, Chhaya went with her mother to the adjoining room. The hands of the clock ticked on, and with every passing hour she became more certain that the marriage would not take place. She was not feeling well, it was as though someone was knocking against her head, asking for permission to enter. She tried to ignore the pounding, but it was relentless, making her cringe in agony. The pressure became unbearable, sweat poured from her temples, neck and back. Her heart sank. 'Please, please leave me alone,' she murmured.

'We can't do that, little dulhan, just turn, I will tuck the saree in from the back,' the beautician, Mala, said.

Chhaya heard her, but the voice seemed to come from far away. She had not even realised that she had spoken aloud.

Mala was worried about the bride. Perhaps she was not feeling well, or maybe she had a lover and didn't want to get married? She had dressed so many brides, she could read their minds just by looking at them. As she watched the beads of sweat pour down the bride's forehead, she knew that the girl was scared.

The beautician tried her best to make the girl feel at ease by chatting with her, but she did not reply even once. She did mutter some words now and then, but they made no sense to Mala. Feeling uneasy, the beautician turned the submissive form of the bride towards her to adjust the pallu of the saree. When her hands accidentally touched the uncovered midriff of the girl, it was wet and sticky. Startled, she looked at the face of the bride and was shocked to see that her face was dripping with sweat. Her eyes were tightly closed and she had started swaying slowly as if in a trance.

Alarmed, Mala made the girl sit on the bed and then lie down. Then she quickly ran out to call for help. When Chhaya's father saw the beautician he knew that something had happened to his daughter.

A doctor was called. While he checked her, the family members crowded into the room looking at the chalk-white face of the unconscious girl. The beautician bolted the door from inside—the baraat was expected to reach the house soon.

The veins in Chhaya's forehead were throbbing visibly, as if they were trying to burst from under her skin. She was so wet with sweat that it looked as if she had been dipped in water.

'He Bhagwan! Please save her, doctor sahib, please do something,' her grandmother wailed.

'There was something really wrong with her, not with her health, but something else. It was as if she was possessed, as if she was talking to someone, when I ran to call you,' the beautician said to Chhaya's mother, who was caressing her daughter's forehead, tears flowing down her cheeks. 'As if she was trying to plead with someone...'

'What do you mean? Is there any sense in what you are saying?' Chhaya's father said, glaring at the beautician.

'I don't know how to explain what I mean, but it was—'

'—Please be quiet! She is regaining consciousness. Everything will be okay,' the doctor interrupted them. He too was puzzled. The physical examination showed nothing abnormal, but the bride's whole form—the white face, the tightly clenched fists, the sweat—gave a different picture.

'Will she be able to sit through the marriage, doctor? The baraat will arrive soon,' the girl's mother asked.

'Yes. Give her sometime. Whatever it was, it seems to have passed. Her breathing is returning to normal. She just needs to rest. I'll give her some glucose,' the doctor said, adding, 'Please, everyone leave the room, give her some air. Only the parents should stay here.'

A few moments after everyone had left the room, Chhaya opened her eyes. There was still fear and helplessness in them. She slowly closed them again.

Mala, who had stayed back, started moving quietly to the door.

'You will be fine Chhaya, don't worry, everything is okay. There is still time for the baraat, you will be okay by then,' her father said gently. Chhaya opened her eyes again, and this time there was only sadness. Tears silently trickled down from the sides.

'I saw him Papa, he came to me. It was the first time that he was angry,' she said softly, barely audible. The beautician stopped. No one spoke.

'He was not angry with me but the person I was going to marry. He ranted and screamed "no one will marry her, she is mine".' Chhaya began to sob. 'He is dead Papa, I saw him die. He was entering the car when he collapsed. I saw it all.'

No one moved. Everyone stared at her in shock.

'I saw him too, he was sitting in the car smiling. And then he saw me. I was scared but then my fear disappeared and there was love as he stroked my head. He said we will always be together because we love each other. No one will take me away, he will always be there to guard me,' she finished with an effort, crying uncontrollably.

A soft knock broke the spell. It was Mala who opened the door.

It was the doctor. 'There has been some bad news,' he said to Chhaya's parents. 'It would be better if you come out. Let the bride, no, the girl, rest.'

Ghosts Don't Exist

During my months of travel in and around Shimla, I encountered various people. Once I even met a girl who was visiting Shimla for a similar reason to mine. She too was interested in the supernatural, specifically ghosts that wander around cemeteries. This is her story.

♦

'Excuse me, can you tell me where the cemetery is?' I asked a woman at the local bus stop near St. Bedes' College.

'Cemetery? I'm not sure, I think it is in that direction,' she said, pointing towards a narrow road.

'There are some houses ahead on that road. Maybe you should ask someone there, they...' the last part of her reply was drowned out by the approach of a bus. The woman disappeared inside it after I had thanked her.

The promised houses were nowhere in sight even after a walk of about ten minutes on the narrow meandering road. Finally, after another ten minutes, I turned a blind curve and saw, to my relief, a couple of houses. I rang the bell at the door of the first building.

A visibly irritated middle-aged woman opened the door and barked, 'Yes?'

'I'm sorry to have disturbed you, I just wanted to ask for directions to the cemetery.'

'There are no cemeteries here,' she said, and shut the door with bang.

How rude! I thought, wondering about all the stories I had heard about people in the town being very friendly. I went on ahead, and five minutes later I found myself in an open square with half a dozen shops and a few houses. Some people were lounging around, making the most of the sun.

I went up to an old man, and, now a little unsure about how I would be received, asked hesitantly, 'Excuse me, if you don't mind, I am trying to locate a cemetery. I have been told it is somewhere near here.'

'Hmm, it's a very old cemetery, you want to go there?'
'Yes, how far is it from here?'
'Not very far. Go straight down this road, you'll see it after about fifteen minutes on your left. It's a small cemetery: very old, no more in use.'

'Thank you,' I beamed.

'But what are you going to do there? The chowkidar is not there. Are you alone? Don't you have someone with you?' he asked, looking a little concerned.

'No, it's just me. Is it unsafe? Have you heard any stories about the place, I mean ghostly ones?' I asked with interest.

The old man laughed, a dry cackling laugh. 'Ghosts! No one sees them now, their days are over. It was in the past that people used to meet them, but not anymore,' he said and then added, 'I have not heard any story, I was just thinking that you are a young girl and there is very little traffic on this road.'

'Where does the road lead to?'

'It goes on to meet the Sanjauli–Chhota Shimla Road, the National Highway. But it takes more than half an hour to reach the highway, and generally the local buses do not stop there.'

I nodded my head. 'I will just have a look around and then return by this route and catch the bus from Navbahar Chowk,' I said.

The old man shook his head and murmured, 'The things that young people do. We cannot understand them.' He then turned back to what he had been doing before I'd gone up to him: gazing at his feet clad in woollen socks! And I can't understand the older generation, I chuckled to myself.

It was nearly noon by this time. I checked my watch and thought that I could be back in an hour to have my packed lunch of butter and cheese sandwiches.

The slight breeze blowing lifted my mood. I started humming a Hindi film song, softly in the beginning and then loudly as I walked down the road. I could afford to do so as there was no one around. After several blind curves I saw the cemetery. It was on a small hillock. The main cemetery was an enclosed area; its boundary wall made up of stones. There were about sixty graves, well structured with a cemented path in between. Several names and dates were faintly visible from where I stood outside the boundary wall. The whole area was surrounded with a thick forest of deodar, kail and oak trees.

I spent about half an hour strolling around the peaceful place, recollecting the words of the old man who had given me directions to the cemetery: 'There are no ghosts now, ghosts existed long back.' Without any real reason I laughed loudly. Having had a proper look around the place, I decided to return. As I walked down the road, I saw someone ahead of me, walking in the same direction. Good! At least I would have company, I told myself as I hurried to catch up with him.

'Excuse me, I am also going this way, do you mind if I join you?' I said as I walked alongside him.

'Not at all. What are you doing here?' he asked in a soft and musical voice.

'Oh nothing. I was just strolling around the cemetery. Isn't it strange?' I said and then stopped. He silently walked on ahead. I started off again to make myself clear, 'I mean, so many people have lived before us and now they are all gone, dead, their bodies buried in the earth. Life is so strange. Isn't it?'

'Yes, it is strange,' he said softly, almost as if he were talking to himself.

'You live nearby?'

'Yes, quite nearby.'

'So you are coming from that bifurcation where the road meets the Sanjauli–Chota Shimla one. How far is that road from here?'

'Not far, it will suit you.'

'Oh, I am not interested in going from there. For one thing, I don't know the way back from there; secondly, I've heard the local buses do not stop there. Thirdly, I have decided to have my lunch at one of the shops ahead.'

'You seem to be quite well planned.'

'Hardly planned! In fact I am the worst of planners. You know, I have been planning to write a book on strange tales since long but I have made the start today only. God only knows how much time it's going to take...' on and on I blabbered without even bothering to look at my companion. Soon I saw the shops.

'Good! We have reached so soon, it was so nice talking to you, time flew so fast. By the way, I am...' I turned towards him.

I stopped dead. There was no one with me. For a moment I was confused. I looked around, but it was clear that the man had vanished. Shocked and trembling with fear I ran towards the bright sunlight and the shops.

I stopped at the first shop I came across, and, mustering all my strength, looked back at the road from where I had come. It was still empty.

'Beta, when you went away, I remembered a rumour that circulates here. A man with a soft and musical voice roams on the patch between here and the cemetery. Many people have come across him. They say he gives you company if you are alone. Interestingly, no one remembers his personality or his face.... But it is all foolish talk. There are no ghosts here. Did you find the cemetery? How was your experience?' the old man asked as I sat on a stool to steady my trembling legs.

The Walk Back

Ranjit Singh looked affectionately at his friend. Forty years had passed since they had last met, and this was only a chance meeting. In fact, had it not been for the owner of Maria Bookstore on the Mall, where they had both been browsing, they would not have recognised each other. Mr Sood's comment as to how relaxed Amandeep must be feeling after his long tenure as Ambassador in Latin America and Europe had drawn the retired Colonel's attention.

Ranjit had come to Shimla on holiday, wanting to visit the town where he had spent his childhood, and the former Ambassador was there to deliver a lecture on international relations.

'It's difficult to believe that so many years have passed since we left school,' the Colonel said.

'Yes, and that we were children once, brimming with energy,' said Amandeep. 'Let's spend the evening together. I'm leaving tomorrow,' he added placing his hand on his friend's shoulder. 'I am staying at the Cecil. Join me there. We will drink, dine and relive the bygone days.'

Later that evening the two friends relaxed together, sitting cross-legged on the cushioned settee of the Cecil suite.

'You know, I'm enjoying my drink after a long time. It's nice not to have to drink quickly in order to move to the next party or to work,' Amandeep said.

'Is it so! Well, I always make sure I can enjoy my drinks!' the Colonel said with a twinkle in his eye. 'Come on, let's make a toast to future meetings!' Having filled both their glasses with the golden liquid, the Colonel continued. 'I always wanted to ask you, but never had the opportunity: did you or did you not kiss that English girl who had come from England with her brother to see his old school?'

'So you want to know whether I had kissed her or not? Well, yes, I did kiss her,' Amandeep said, his face red.

The Colonel laughed loudly, shaking his head.

'What is it? You don't believe me?' Amandeep was indignant as he gulped his drink down in one go.

'No, I don't! You are lying, you were always that lecherous kind as far as looking at girls was concerned, but when it came to the practical part, even initiating a conversation with girls was an uphill task!' he said teasingly.

'I'm telling you the truth! It was you who said let's share secrets and now you don't believe me!' Amandeep said in a hurt tone.

'All right. Tell me where did you kiss her? In the library?'

'No, it was not in the library. You remember that small nook in the main building? The one from where you could see anyone coming from either side of the corridor, but you yourself could remain undetected? I remember how all of you were jealous that she liked me. And the best part was, it was *she* who stopped and stared at me with those doleful, innocent eyes. I tried to resist, after all I was the escort and she was a guest of the school, but she was very persistent,' Amandeep said musingly.

'Another peg for you?' Colonel asked, and without waiting for a reply poured his friend another drink.

The former Ambassador watched his friend and decided to ask him something he had always wanted to. He hoped that Ranjit would tell the truth. After all, they were old men now, not afraid of ghosts any longer. That incident had been whispered about for months in the school dormitories after lights had been switched off.

'Okay, now it's time for your true confession,' Amandeep began.

The Colonel looked up enquiringly.

Amandeep hesitated, and then, curiosity getting the better of him, he carried on. 'What happened to you before you were found unconscious that night in school?' he asked.

There was silence in the room.

'You don't want to talk about it?' Amandeep asked softly. He only had sketchy details of that incident. The watchman had found his friend lying unconscious in the corridor leading to the library. Ranjit had been moved to the sick room, where he'd stayed for more than two days. No one had been allowed to visit him except for the Principal and the Matron. Later his parents had taken away, and he'd only returned to school after a month. By that time exams had been only a few weeks away: everyone had been so busy with their studies that Ranjit's return had gone largely unnoticed. The few questions that had come his way he'd ignored. However, there had been a rumour that Ranjit had had an encounter with a ghost.

Now, almost four decades after the incident, Ranjit decided to tell his friend what had happened.

◆

It was our outing day and I had just watched the late afternoon movie show at the Ritz with two of our classmates. We were on our way back from school when I suddenly had a great urge to relieve myself. The school gate was about 200 metres ahead; I asked my friends to carry on and walked into the jungle. Remember how the thick the deodar jungle was? I was standing near one of the trees, when a few seconds later, out of the corner of my eye, I noticed something white coming towards me. Embarrassed, I tried to warn whoever was coming of my presence. Twice I coughed loudly and even thumped my left leg on the ground. But the white form—I could now vaguely make out that it was a man with one hand stretched out—kept moving towards me.

Hoping it was not someone from the school, I watched as the person came closer. The man's face was not visible. In fact, oddly enough, there seemed to be nothing above the shoulder. Perhaps it was someone very dark? I thought, straining now to get a better look. Then my eyes shifted to the man's outstretched hand. And there, in the man's palm, was a head!

I panicked. There was a headless man holding the silver-haired head of an Englishman coming towards me! I opened my mouth and screamed as loudly as I could. I was terrified! I just shut my eyes, waiting to be attacked or devoured. A few seconds passed. Nothing happened. Slowly I opened my eyes and forced myself to look at the place where I had seen the man. There was nothing except for the trees! I looked all around me. No one was there.

The Walk Back 107

Where had the thing vanished? Was it my imagination? It couldn't be. I was sure I had seen something. I stumbled out of the forest and ran as fast as I could to the main gate of the school.

◆

Ranjit stopped and there was a long silence.

Amandeep looked at the chalk-white face of his friend and noticed his hands were shaking. He poured another drink for both of them and handed one to the Colonel.

Ranjit had never been able to forget that night; even now, after so long, his mouth was dry with fear. He gulped down the drink and said, 'I had to be admitted into a psychiatric ward for a month. I had lost my voice.'

'Sorry old chap, I never knew,' Amandeep said sympathetically. 'I had heard about other ghosts in the school, but never about this one.'

'Other ghosts? What other ones?' the Colonel asked bewildered.

'I mean the other little rumours that circulated in the school about these unknown people. One was about an English boy whose name was Stalk. He had made a makeshift laboratory underground. He was so good in science, that he had designed a gadget whereby a red bulb flickered if someone came in the vicinity.

He died during one of his experiments. Many boys claimed to have come across his spirit, while several others have heard his footsteps underneath the floor board.'

'Yes, yes. I remember now. There was one story about a boy who died in the chemistry lab while performing an experiment. Apparently his spirit used to visit the lab at night,' the Colonel said.

'Do you remember the rumour about the Briton who rode his horse around the school grounds on moonlit nights?'

'Yes. And how, after midnight, a lot of noises would come from the kitchen: someone walking, washing utensils and the clatter of crockery. But when the kitchen door was opened, there would be no one inside!' the Colonel said.

'And that story relating to Mr Sharma, the English teacher. Once, at midnight, he heard some noise outside his room. When he opened the door, he saw an English woman who passed him and then disappeared in the darkness.'

'I wonder if these stories circulate in the school even now?' the former Ambassador said.

'I wonder too,' said the Colonel, as he poured himself another stiff drink.

The Grave of an English Lady

'This is the bifurcation,' Kalpana said pointing to the right. Sania, their one-year-old daughter was sleeping peacefully in her lap.

'Yes, you still remember,' he said, turning off the National Highway onto the road she had pointed out.

'How can I forget?'

Yes, how could they forget that trip they had made almost two years back? He could remember every minute detail of that trip.

◆

'Dagshai! Are you sure you want to go there? Why don't you go to Kasauli? It's a nice small hill town.

There are a number of hotels there. Most of the tourists go there,' the man blabbered.

Kalpana looked at her husband. Why didn't he say something instead of just sitting there quietly? Did it no longer matter to him? Was he blind to her unhappiness?

'Where exactly do you want to go madam?' the man asked again.

'Dagshai, as she said. Could you tell us which road to take?' Rohit asked politely.

'About four or five kilometres ahead is a bifurcation; the road to the right will take you to Dagshai. You are coming from where? Chandigarh? Delhi?' he asked.

'We are from Mumbai. Your place Himachal is very beautiful, so cool and clean,' Rohit said, and restarted the vehicle. Kalpana sighed with relief. She just wanted to get to Dagshai; she didn't want to have to handle a stranger's questions and advice.

Rohit was a marketing executive in a multinational company. He had had to come to Delhi for official work. His wife had accompanied him, and they had decided to take a week off. He had hired a company car for the trip.

'This must be the bifurcation,' murmured Rohit as he turned off the National Highway.

'Put on some music, some nice peppy songs,' he said, glancing at his wife. She did not respond. He knew that he would have to repeat everything he said;

when she got like this on these trips, she was too preoccupied with her thoughts to listen to anything around her.

They had been married ten years now. They married young, in fact, they had eloped. The first few years of their marriage had been bliss. The trouble had started with their inability to have a child. The years rolled by, and her unhappiness only increased. Rohit did not mind so much about not having children. As long as they were happy and loved each other, he thought, he would be content. In the beginning, there were some depressing moments, but they were able to be there for each other. But gradually things started deteriorating. Anger, tears, arguments and shouting started overshadowing everything else.

The situation worsened when she started visiting temples, tantriks and sadhus. She offered prayers at every possible place in and around Mumbai. She became convinced that she would be able to conceive only through a miracle. The stronger her belief grew, the more pressure there was on their marriage. She wanted to make pilgrimages to holy towns, and it was difficult for him to get leave all the time. His work suffered and he took out his frustration and anger at home; this in turn culminated in her having bouts of depression that lasted for days.

She accused him of not understanding what she was going through. Rohit did understand her overwhelming desire to have a child, but tried to convince her that having a baby was insignificant compared to their relationship.

Their marriage was dying. He had grown older before time, becoming more temperamental. She had become cranky. But he still loved her and knew that she loved him. So he tried to bring things back to normal; with every passing day, however, this was becoming difficult.

A few weeks back, when she had suggested this ludicrous deity—a *ghost*—he had seriously considered that her obsession had finally driven her crazy. Later, on reflection, the idea appealed to him. Perhaps, after visiting the tomb or whatever of the ghost, they could spend some time together. It would be a change for both of them and it would do them good to have a quiet holiday. He had never been to Himachal, but had heard that it was a beautiful hill state. Besides, he was quite relieved not to have to touch the feet of yet another tantrik, baba or sadhu. He had made her promise that after fulfilling her part of the agenda, they would explore the hills for a few days and enjoy their holiday on his terms. Kalpana had said that she would try. He hoped she would.

The air was cool as the couple drove on. The view was cheery: little hillocks dotted the road on either side of the car. Rohit checked his rear-view mirror, there was no vehicle behind him. He concentrated on the small road with its many blind curves and pine forests. At a few points, the ascent was so steep that he feared the vehicle would slide backwards. Thankfully, despite its huffing and puffing, the car managed the climb. At every curve he pressed the horn and then craned his neck to look for any oncoming vehicles. He was sure that, if something did come, there would be no space for both of them to pass on this narrow road.

'How far is it?' asked Kalpana, her face showing her anxiety. They had never travelled on such a narrow and dangerous road before.

'I don't know, that man said it was just a few kilometres,' he said.

'Rohit! This is beautiful!'

Surprised, he looked at her and then out her window. He stopped the vehicle and took in the scenery. It was breathtaking. By now, they had driven up to a considerable height. He could see the National Highway coiling its way amongst the hills like a long snake. Opposite them was another mountain top, with a temple on its peak, perhaps it was Kasauli. Down below he saw small green terraces and little cottages scattered here and there, surrounded by small green pine trees. The sky sparkled and twinkled in its blueness, covering everything that lay beneath it.

'I have never seen anything so beautiful,' Rohit said as he put his arm around his wife's shoulder.

'Hmm,' she said and snuggled close to him. Her body warmth seeped into him and he realised that it was cold. Cold weather in September! What luxury!

'Where is the shawl that you packed?'

'Why?'

'Honey, it's cold. Look you're even shivering!'

'No I am not,' Kalpana laughed as she straightened.

Time suspended as they looked intently into each other's eyes.

'I love you. Thank you for doing all this for me,' she said softly as her eyes welled up with tears.

'Me too,' he replied, hugging her.

Rohit started the car and they moved on again.

'What are you thinking?' he asked after some time.

'I am thanking God that we haven't come across another vehicle on this narrow road!' she said.

'I think we've finally reached!'

'Where?'

'Dagshai silly. I think this road goes round the whole town or village for that matter. Ah! Here's a shop, let's ask someone,' he said, parking the vehicle on the side of the road.

The owner of the groceries shop they walked up to greeted them heartily. After he had ascertained that they did, in fact, want to be in Dagshai, the man eagerly related the little town's history. For an hour he told them of how Dagshai used to be a thriving, beautiful cantonment till Independence, when the

National Highway was rerouted, by-passing Dagshai. The number of visitors dropped; the Army battalion was converted into a public school further reducing the population besides leading to a loss of cantonment status. Over time, the town had become the deserted place it now was, except for the summers when a few tourists visited it to walk through its once very busy bazaar. In fact, some of the shops and houses constructed before Independence had never been used.

'It can be developed into an attractive tourist spot if the roads are widened and improved and some offices opened to boost the population and thus provide work. There is no doubt about the beauty of this place. It has such good climate and such a beautiful landscape,' said Rohit, sipping his tea.

'Anyway, now you young people can go around and see it for yourself. Don't mind me, I am an old man who loves talking about its history,' the shop owner told them.

Rohit could feel Kalpana's eyes boring into him, pleading him to ask the man about what they had specifically come there for.

Hesitantly, he began, 'It was nice to find out about Dagshai's history. We are grateful to you for devoting so much time informing us about the place. Actually, we have come for a different reason. If you could help us...'

The old man looked at him and raised his eyebrows. He shifted his gaze to the woman beside him. He sensed her nervousness as she kept her gaze fixed on the empty glass of tea in her hand. He wondered, could it be that they...

'Yes? What else can I tell you?' he asked politely.

Rohit looked at Kalpana, who stared back at him silently. Underneath the table she was clutching his hand tight.

The old man waited patiently. He was now sure.

'Uncle, we have been married for a long time and we...we...' the woman stopped and looked at her husband for support.

'She means to say, that we do not have any children. Someone told her that there is a ghost or spirit who helps couples in conceiving,' he blurted out. 'I don't believe in it, but for her sake I don't mind trying,' he added hastily.

The old man said nothing.

Rohit turned his face towards the open window. He felt embarrassed and uncomfortable. This is what happens when you ask people about the whereabouts of a ghost who helps in conceiving babies! he thought.

'I have never heard of any such ghost here,' the old man said at last.

'You mean there is no such thing?' the woman asked in despair.

The Grave of an English Lady 117

'No, there is no such *ghost*,' he said. And then added lightly, 'I think you are referring to mem ki kabar.'

Rohit pressed Kalpana's hand as he watched her expression change from despair to hope again.

'Well, perhaps that is what it is. What exactly is it?' he asked the old man.

'Do you know what "mem ki kabar" means?'

'Grave of a lady?'

'In a way, yes, the grave of a mem, an *English* lady.'

And with baited breath the couple listened to the story of the English lady.

◆

At the beginning of the twentieth century, a young British air force officer was posted at Dagshai. He came along with his wife. The couple were obviously very much in love. About a month later, they found out she was pregnant and they were ecstatic. The couple had fallen in love with Dagshai and despite advice from friends and colleagues, they decided to have their baby in Dagshai. However, as the day of the delivery approached, the lady began to feel unwell.

When her labour pains began, she was rushed to the doctor's house. Unfortunately both the lady and the baby died during childbirth. They were buried in the town's graveyard.

The shattered officer was sent to England on personal request—Dagshai had given him so much love and then snatched away the most precious thing of his life. He returned after a few months with a ten-feet long marble statue of a woman lying down and a small child standing behind her head, gazing down lovingly at her. This marble statue was fixed on the grave of the lady. On the tombstone was inscribed: Mary Rebecca Weston and our unborn child, December 10, 1909. The officer then returned to his country. Now, even after ninety years, the grave was still there, although it was in a dilapidated condition.

♦

When the old man stopped talking, he saw Kalpana was crying quietly; her husband too seemed to be touched by the story.

After a short pause, Rohit asked the man, 'But what has this to do with the power of the spirit to help couples have a child?'

'Perhaps it's a myth or may be it's the truth, I don't know. I just know that many couples come here for this reason. Earlier, it was just the locals, but now people have started coming from as far as Chennai and Kerala to be blessed by the Lady. It is said that if you keep a little piece of marble or soil from the mem ki kabar in your house, you are sure to be blessed with a child.'

'I knew it, we have come to the right place,' said Kalpana, tears still rolling down her cheeks.

'If there is any truth in the story, the mem's spirit will help you, beti. It will guard over you and your child and see to it that no harm comes to either of you,' the old man said getting up.

'When did this belief start, I mean childless couples coming here?' asked Rohit, as he also rose.

'I am not sure about that. It is said that a unit of the Bihar regiment started the practice. The only sad thing is that, earlier, the marble statue was a masterpiece. Now it is in a bad shape, first because it got broken in the riots of 1947, and then later because of the little pieces that are being taken by childless couples to their homes.'

'Thank you. We are very grateful for your help and for your time,' said Kalpana.

'Mention not, you are just like my children. Come I will show you the way. I pray that you get what you came for.'

The Prince with the Red Rose

Maria was very excited. She was finally in Shimla, about to begin studying in her dream school. She had come all the way from Rajasthan just to be here. For almost half an hour she had been walking around the school campus, located in a picturesque spot amidst thick deodar trees. Her legs and feet were both aching, but her heart was bursting with joy and excitement. She rested her back on the rough surface of a deodar tree and gazed up at the school building. She had read somewhere that it had been constructed in 1864 by the British. It was beautiful, with flowers hanging from every nook and corner. It looked more like the venue of a flower show than a school!

'What are you doing here?'

'Nothing...nothing ma'am. Just looking around,' Maria blurted straightening herself.

The Sister stared hard at the girl. Slim, short hair, black almond-shaped eyes, high cheekbones, a shapely mouth.

'In which standard are you? I have never seen you before.'

'I am new madam. I'll be joining eighth standard.'

'Well, you should be in hostel right now, not wandering around the grounds. And the word madam is not used here.'

Sister Helene looked at her watch, it was ten minutes to four o' clock. 'Run along now, it's your tea time. I hope you are not feeling homesick: if you are, it is always better to stay with your friends and your classmates, rather than be alone,' she said as she walked towards the administrative block.

'Yes ma'm, sorry Sister. But I am not homesick,' she said.

Amused, Sister Helene glanced back at the girl and saw that her eyes were shining with excitement.

'That's good. Run along now,' she said, and watched the girl turn towards the concrete path leading to the hostel.

'God bless you,' the Sister murmured as she went her way, thinking, I hope she doesn't bring trouble with those looks!

Maria was on her way to the hostel when she saw an old man pottering among the plants.

'Hello uncle, I am Maria, from Jodhpur. I am new here,' she said tentatively to the old man, whose back was towards her.

'You are no longer new here. It's been more than a week since the school opened,' he answered gruffly.

Maria squatted and touched the plants as gently as possible.

'That is true, but to me everything is so new and beautiful.'

Her happy tone could not be ignored; the old man looked at the girl. A pretty child, he thought.

'Maria—that's what you said your name was, no?—most of the new girls are homesick, but not you. That's good,' he said.

'You are the second person who has mentioned homesickness. I am so excited to be here: alone and independent!'

'I am glad beta, that you have found this place enchanting. Er, don't keep touching that plant, the bud may break off,' he added.

Maria let go of the delicate orange and yellow leafed plant, which she had been trying to straighten. She hadn't even noticed that there was a bud on it.

'Sorry uncle, I will be on my way. It is going to be tea time soon.'

'Yes, you better get going. If you are interested in flowers, trees, plants, come to me again, I will tell you all about them.'

'Thank you, I'm sure I'll meet you soon.'

'In which class did you say you were in?'

'I don't think I did say: I'm in the eighth standard,' she said as she hurried off towards the hostel. The gardener thoughtfully looked at her receding figure.

'God bless you child,' he murmured as he bent down and started working on his plants again.

'Hey! Where in hell were you? If you hadn't returned in another five minutes, I would have come looking for you!' her friend Manveen, whom she met near the hostel entrance, said.

'I was just looking around the campus...'

'Are you crazy? You're not allowed to roam around like that. You're supposed to be in the hostel after school hours,' Manveen said indignantly as they both entered the hostel.

'Silly, I didn't leave the campus. Can't a person look around one's own school? Don't be so shocked! Anyway, I was caught by a ma'am, no Sister, while hanging around near the administrative building,' she said, giggling loudly.

'You really are mad! No wonder Meena told me to take care of you.' Meena was the head girl of the school, and by 'take care' she had meant 'keep an eye'. Just like any other boarding school, here too the older girls were concerned that the new entrants be able to adjust and mingle with the others easily. Sometimes it took newcomers a year to feel at home in the school. It seemed that Maria would be an exception, though. She was already friendly with nearly all the girls in her class.

'Now hurry up, put on your cardigan. Let's go to the Mess for tea,' Manveen said. A few minutes later they were at the Mess. Manveen went to talk to some of her other friends so Maria sat alone at one of the tables. Meena, the head girl, came up to her. 'I heard you disappeared again? We were about to send someone to look for you,' she told Maria.

'I'm sorry. I was just looking around the school complex. I met Manveen on the way, she told me you were, er, worried.'

'Well, be careful of the rules the next time.'

'Do you like Shimla and this school?' Maria asked the head girl, trying to change the subject.

'Like? I've never thought of it like that. It's not bad, we get used to it. For us the school is a second home.'

'Hmm. What about Shimla? The beauty, hills and lush greenery?'

'Well, it's nice. I belong to Chopal, about five hours from here. For me, Chopal is much more beautiful,' said Meena.

'Hi Meena. The meeting is tonight?' a senior from the tenth standard came up to them and asked.

'Ya. Be there in my room.'

'What meeting?' asked Maria.

'To welcome the prince. The "day" has come early,' said the girl, whose name Maria did not know.

'Shut up...you know you're not supposed to talk about it openly in the Mess,' Meena turned around and said angrily.

'Oops! Sorry! Come on Meena, be a sport. No one heard except for her and she'll probably be there too,' she said, looking at Maria.

'It is I who decides who is to be invited and who will not.'

'Don't be so bossy!' the girl chided, moving away.

Baffled, Maria looked at the head girl. Meena didn't say a word; abruptly she got up and left the Mess. What were they talking about? Maria wondered. What was this mysterious meeting?

There was still some minutes left for the evening studies to finish when the whispering started. Maria had already finished her day's work and was flicking mindlessly through the pages of her English book when the girls around her began to talk in low voices about the meeting later on. Where would it take place? What would the agenda be? she could hear them asking each other.

'I know, I know. I will keep it in my room, and take my advice, use the eyeliner rather than that filthy black polish.'

'Why don't you all listen to Shree? There is sense in what she is saying.'

'Sh...sh...Make sure Sister Helene does not hear.' Maria recognised the voice: it was Manveen.

'Don't be stupid. Sister knows about it. In fact she has known about it for the last twenty years! You were not even born then!' Shree said.

'Shhh...can't you speak softly!' Manveen said as the girls giggled.

'What about the sixth standard girls?' one voice asked.

'What about them? You know this starts from seventh standard onwards,' Shree replied.

Just then the bell rang. The girls filed out, most of them heading out to the playground. Maria went too. She wanted to ask someone what they had been talking about. She looked around for Manveen but couldn't spot her anywhere. She went up to Shree and asked, 'What were you all discussing?'

'What do you mean?'

'About some meeting? Using boot polish and eyeliner...I didn't understand anything.'

'Oh! That! I don't know whether I am allowed to tell you. After all you are not yet one of us.'

'Keep it to yourself then, I am not even interested,' Maria snapped and joined a group of girls playing basketball.

Shree vindictively made up her mind not to let the new girl know about their secret just now. The day—Friday the thirteenth—had come early this year. Usually November came first, and by then they were comfortable enough to tell the new girls about it. She would tell the other girls, especially the bossy Meena, that Maria might laugh at their faces and make a joke of it. She'd tell Maria later of course...she'd see what they were doing anyway. Let her come to me and ask me again, Shree thought.

Maria didn't sleep well and the next day she woke up with a headache and a slight fever. No one had invited her for the meeting yet and she felt rejected. On Meena's advice she went to the sick room in the afternoon where the Sister gave her two pills to swallow and told her to lie down for some time. Maria dozed off and by the time the Sister woke her up, it was evening.

'Have your milk and biscuits.'

'What time is it, Sister?'

'Nearly seven o' clock, finish your milk. I will come back and take your temperature.'

Maria gulped down the milk. She was famished.

'Got ill so soon? Thought you were an energetic girl.'

Startled Maria looked around.

'I'm here.' The voice was coming from the window. She turned and saw the gardener.

'Hello uncle. How are you? How did you know I was here?' she asked in her usual chirpy manner.

'I was working on this ivy, when I saw you gulping down the food,' he said with a twinkle in his eye.

'I hadn't had anything since morning. I did not sleep well yesterday, but now I am feeling all right. They'll let me leave the sick room, won't they?' she asked.

'Hmm. What about today? Will you be able to sleep? The day has come early this year.'

Surprised, Maria was about to ask the gardener what he was talking about when she heard the Sister coming down the corridor.

'Who are you talking to young lady? Come, we will check your fever now,' the Sister said.

Maria smiled and looked towards the window, but there was no one there. The gardener had left.

She had her dinner in the sick room and an hour later was allowed to go to her dormitory. As she approached the room, she could hear a lot of noise coming from within.

'What are you doing, standing in the middle! Move yaar,' a senior said, pushing her aside as she entered along with two other girls. Maria stood stupefied. All the girls in the room were dressed shabbily, and all of them had their hair hanging around their faces, uncombed and tangled. But this was nothing compared to what they had done to their faces.

'What's going on?' she asked no one in particular.

'Come on! Change into your dirtiest night-suit quickly. Or wear a mismatching one. There is the eyeliner and the black polish, the rouge...Whatever you want, put it on,' said Meena.

Shocked Maria looked at the head girl. Half her face was blackened, she had smeared lipstick all over her mouth and chin, and it looked as if she had sprinkled talcum powder on her hair. She was wearing a crushed blue top with striped purple and red pyjamas.

Maria looked around her. This was absurd...what was wrong with all of them? All the girls had painted their faces black, blue and red. The beautiful Paharan girls, with their peaches and cream complexions, had made themselves look ugly, and the strangest thing was that they were all so happy about it, laughing, giggling and making all kinds of faces.

'What is going on?' she asked again, feeling helpless. Perhaps it was some strange kind of theme party? She felt left out, she didn't know what to do.

A stern knock on the door made most of the girls scramble to their beds.

'Lights off,' the Sister called from outside.

The bewildered Maria watched some of the girls sneak out to go to their own dormitories.

'Hurry up, switch off the light and get into your bed silly, before Sister comes in,' hissed Shree. Maria still stood like a statue near the switchboard, undecided and confused.

'Lights off, I said!' the Sister called from the corridor loudly.

Maria fumbled with the switch, turned it off, found her bed—third from right—and lay down. It was really not her day! First the sick room and then this hurricane.

'Remember to use that eyeliner,' she heard someone call out to her, before sleep overcame her. The next thing she knew, the shrill six o' clock morning bell was ringing. Stretching, she saw that most of the girls were already awake. Surprised, she looked around and noticed that girls from other dormitories were there too. Either they were scrubbing their faces, or helping someone clean up.

'Will someone tell me what this was all about,' Maria asked loudly.

Some of the girls turned to look at her.

'Oh no...look...' one of the girls said, ashen faced. The other girls in the room stopped what they were doing. Slowly, a hush filled the room as they all looked towards Maria.

'What is it? What are you looking at?' Maria asked, looking at the sea of faces in front of her. She felt she was going crazy.

Slowly, one of the girls pointed towards her bed.

Maria turned to look where she was pointing. Behind her, lying on her pillow—she did not know how she had not noticed it before—was a red rose on her pillow. Slowly, as if controlled by something beyond themselves, all the girls walked closer to Maria and her bed. There was fear in their eyes, she saw, as they looked at her and then at the rose. Maria's heart sank; she felt a chill creeping down her spine.

Finally one of them spoke.

'The dead prince has chosen you.'

'What...what are you saying?'

'Why didn't you make yourself look ugly? Look, he has left his token of love—the red rose—on your bed!' a girl said, pointing towards the rose.

'I don't understand... I don't know what you are talking about!' Maria said, her voice edged with hysteria.

Manveen walked up to her. 'Maria, every year, on thirteenth November or Friday the thirteenth, whichever comes earlier, the ghost of an English prince comes riding on a horse to the school. He leaves a rose on the bed of whichever girl he finds pretty. That is why, on this night, all the girls from seventh standard onwards make themselves as ugly as possible... After all, who wants to have a spirit as a beloved,' she finished, as Maria swooned, fainting near the bed where lay the fresh red rose.

The Lady on the Rickshaw

The woman adjusted herself on the rickshaw. She was quaintly dressed: a flared peach gown, white gloves, and her face hidden by a delicate embroidered bonnet. Even her mannerisms seemed Victorian.

As the rickshaw entered the Lakkar Bazaar tunnel, she thought about the number of times she had been there. More than a hundred times, surely, she said to herself. And every time nostalgia overtook her. She went back in time not one, two or ten years, but more than a hundred years! The rickshaw trundled on, making a small creaky noise.

As she left the tunnel, she gave a backward glance at the long black hole. The natives had started parking those modern vehicles she hated—the small box-like suffocating four wheelers and ugly, uncomfortable two wheelers—there. Disgusted she turned, and the rickshaw moved on. How could anyone make such abhorrent things! She recalled the motorcars of her time when she visited England: they had such elegance, grace and an air of romance about them! But life had changed since then, she sighed. As the years rolled by, she remained a silent witness to the changes sweeping her Simla. The place had become a slum. Her contemporaries—some of whom she met occasionally—shared her concern and were stunned and shocked by the way things were going in this one-time summer capital of the British Raj.

The conifer and oak forests which had grown thickly around the city during her time, had been decimated to small green patches now. Instead, the slopes were covered by abdominal concrete monsters, the architecture and colours of which had no connection with the ambiance of the town.

The old Victorian houses of her time were no longer there. Most of them had burnt down—Snowdon, Walker Hospital, Kennedy House, Regal...the list was endless. According to the natives, faulty electric wiring and load imbalances had caused the fires, but she knew that their sheer negligence had lead to the collapse of these beautiful buildings.

The rickshaw turned towards the small track leading to Lakkar Bazaar. During her time, this had been a narrow road connecting the Ridge to Sanjauli. She looked with disgust at the dirty shutters of the shops that now lined both sides of the road. Twice she was forced to cover her nose because of the foul smell emanating from large yellow metal boxes overflowing with garbage. She knew that the sewers and drains remained choked most of the time now; heaps of garbage and trash were dumped in all nooks and corners; the streets remained unswept. 'From where did all this filth come,' she muttered sadly, shaking her head. She could not recall Simla having this problem in her time.

Thank God! She had reached the Ridge. It had been one of Simla's only open spaces then, and now it too had changed. There were two large statues: one of Mr Gandhi and the other of Mrs Gandhi. She had heard of Mr Gandhi then, but never of Mrs Gandhi. There was another statue there, and two shops opposite each other with bright, vulgar hoardings in the middle of the Ridge. The open band stand where musicians entertained them—she herself had danced many times there—had been converted into a restaurant now. It looked like a dilapidated outhouse with a huge slanting roof. Very lonely.

It was here on the Ridge that parades were held in honour of the King's birthday on 3 June every year. Underneath the Ridge was the main water reservoir and alongside it the Town Hall had once stood. How shocked everyone had been to discover that the Town Hall was built of inferior stone and that it was crumbling! So, with the exception of the lower portion which housed the Gaiety Theatre, it had been dismantled and it had remained like an ugly scar on the landscape for a long time. She remembered how often they had asked the Engineer-in-Chief to build a new Town Hall as there was no place where a banquet, picture show, meeting or concert could be held except for Davico's dancing hall and restaurant, but all in vain.

As she moved ahead, crossing what was now the Municipal Corporation building, she remembered that kindly lady who had collected funds to provide a shelter for rickshaw coolies, who were forced to suffer so much discomfort during the monsoons. Later the shelter was used as a Municipal Godown.

She stopped at Scandal Point and stared at yet another statue of some leader. How many more were they going to install in this area? she thought.

It was Sir Loius Dane, Lt. Governor of the Punjab, who constructed the carriage road from here round Summer Hill in 1909. She smiled recalling when a very high official inspecting the Summer Hill road in July, came across a subadar with his men working on it. He asked the subadar how long the construction of the road would take.

'Oh! It will not be finished for sometime,' was the reply. 'The regiment does not desire to leave Simla at this season of the year. Therefore, by the Colonel sahib's order, we are working slowly.'

She clutched at her hat which had been about to fall off her head as the rickety carriage moved on to the Mall. It had still retained its European look: the shops looked English even though the names on the hoardings had changed from Messers Bourne & Shepherd, Craddock and De Russet and Messers Hamilton and Co. to Devan Chand Brothers and Baljees.

The Mall, now very wide, was, in the 1870s, an ordinary hill road fit for use only by pedestrians, horses, jhampans and dandies. At many parts of the road, only two horses could go abreast. Then, after a decade, the condition of the Mall improved and jinrickshaws had made their entrance, becoming more popular than the jhampans and dandies.

The jhampan—with its net and satin curtains for protection against the weather—was carried by four coolies and was uncomfortable, while the dandy, consisting of a piece of loose dhurrie fixed by iron rings to a single pole so as to form both seat and footrest was worse. The rider occupied a very undignified position. And then came the jinrickshaws—comfortable, fitted with luxurious cushions, glass windows and rubber tyres, similar to the one in which she was riding. How everybody had felt the change—the authorities and house owners were compelled to widen and improve the roads, which were mere bridle paths.

Suddenly she felt forlorn. Shimla used to be such a picturesque abode at one time but now everything had changed. Enough was enough. Why did her spirit have to come again and again, despite the pain the memories caused her?

'Let us go over to Simla Club,' a voice behind her said.

'Hello. So you too have come today,' she said softly to the man who had appeared by her side. She had not noticed him earlier.

'Do you remember those lights gleaming from the long row of windows in the club? Servants holding horses and jhampanies sitting in groups by their master's chairs clustered around the veranda? Servants hurrying and scurrying in and out to wait on us and our friends coming to dinner from distant bungalows?' he asked.

'Yes...'

'Then the clatter of plates and dishes proclaiming that dinner was nearly ready. Both officers and civilians in every style of Anglo-Indian costume waiting patiently for the signal to fall on. Dinner is announced and we along with our guests file into a large room with a table well laid out with flowers and plated eperques. The servants both of the club and the domestic helpers brought along with each one stand at the back in full attention. Conversation is loud and animated,' he said.

'Why are you quoting what Dr Russell wrote?' she asked, unsure what he was trying to do. He continued as if uninterrupted,

'Cheroots follow closely on the removal of the last Jelly—brandy—Panee, and more wines not very infrequently succeed, while parties are formed and set to work in the inner room and the more jovial of the gentlemen proceed to the execution of vocal pieces such as were wont to be sung in Europe twenty years ago, generally enriched by fine choral effects from the combined strength of all the Company—'

'—Stop, that's enough,' she interrupted. She was not feeling well.

'What's wrong? I am saying all the things you want to hear, think about and dwell on,' he said.

She kept quiet. She told herself to ignore him; he was just an acquaintance, in fact she didn't even know his full name.

'I feel very sad for you, ma'am,' he said softly.

'There is no need to feel sad for me. I think I'll leave now,' she replied haughtily.

'I don't understand you. Most of us went away—body and soul—except those whose spirits wander here because of personal tragedies, as is the case with me. But you...I don't think you went through any tragedy. Look at the way you dress up and come on the rickshaw as if the place were still under the British!' he said.

She turned to go. She didn't want to hear anymore.

'The problem with you ma'am, is that you could not leave your past behind, so you stayed back even after your body died. Your spirit thought it would be the same as before. Unfortunately, or perhaps fortunately, nothing remains the same. Everything changes with time. You have to let go, that is the only salvation for you. Just let go,' he said loudly, as if announcing it to a hundred others.

She could not take any more of it! She hurried away. What did he mean? Did everyone know that her spirit wandered around not because she had suffered from a tragedy, but from an addiction? Yes, it was addiction, an addiction to Simla. It was so deep rooted that nearly a century had passed since she had been there in flesh.

Thoughts of her plight occupied her as she passed the garbage filled boxes that she seen a few hours ago. Down the rickshaw went towards the tunnel. Morose and preoccupied, she didn't see the native standing inside the tunnel trying to start his two-wheeler, until he screamed and then fainted as she passed him.

She was always careful not to use the tunnel in the presence of a mortal, as she was visible only in this stretch. But sometimes you could not help it.